AN INSPECTOR CALLS

Three stories . . . In *An Inspector Calls*, the staff at Primrose Park Community College didn't relish the arrival of the martinet Hayden Staples: school inspector. But could his visit incite murder? In *Looking After Jopo*, Cate agrees to look after her teenage neighbour's baby — only to find herself on the wrong side of a thuggish loan shark. And in *A Village Affair*, Grandmother Grace always finds adventure on her travels and a visit to her lonely daughter is no exception . . .

GERALDINE RYAN

AN INSPECTOR CALLS

Complete and Unabridged

LINFORD
Leicester

First published in Great Britain

First Linford Edition
published 2012

British Library CIP Data

Ryan, Geraldine, *1951* –
   An inspector calls. - -
   (Linford mystery library)
   1. Detective and mystery stories, English.
   2. Large type books.
   I. Title II. Series III. Ryan, Geraldine, *1951* –
   Looking after Jopo. IV. Ryan, Geraldine,
   1951 – Village affair.
   823.9'2–dc23

   ISBN 978–1–4448–1330–2

Published by
F. A. Thorpe (Publishing)
Anstey, Leicestershire

Set by Words & Graphics Ltd.
Anstey, Leicestershire
Printed and bound in Great Britain by
T. J. International Ltd., Padstow, Cornwall

This book is printed on acid-free paper

An Inspector Calls

1

'I'd like to start the day with some good news,' announced Mark Collins. The recently appointed Principal of Primrose Park Community College spoke to a hushed staffroom.

He thought he heard the dour, Scottish science teacher, Alexander Drummond, muttering, 'That'll be the day,' to his neighbour, who happened to be Anna Ziegel, the deputy head. Anna, straight-backed and whippet slim, primped her lips and continued staring forward, making it quite clear to Drummond that the daily staff meeting was no place for wisecracks.

'No, really, it's not all bad,' Mark insisted, beaming nervously.

Drummond raised one shaggy eyebrow and went back to marking the piece of homework on his lap. He couldn't have shown his contempt for Mark's latest innovation of these ten-minute morning briefings more clearly if he'd tried.

Mark knew he should take a leaf out of Anna's book and ignore Drummond's barbed comment instead of trying to butter him up. That was his trouble, though. He longed to be popular. It mattered to him that Drummond — and all the other members of staff who'd been here longer than he had, which was ninety-nine per cent of them — were on his side.

Being new at Primrose Park, he didn't have the confidence of Anna Ziegel, who couldn't have cared less whether the staff liked her or not. He cleared his throat to continue.

'At last night's meeting of the PTA, the Chair announced that the recent Auction of Promises raised enough money to furnish the senior gym with a state-of-the art treadmill and a cross-trainer. The equipment has already been delivered and will be stored safely under lock and key until it can be installed some time next week.'

There were murmurs of pleasure from some quarters — mostly the PE staff, it had to be said. Trish Hayman, who was Head of English and another of the old guard, though considerably more co-operative than Drummond, sat in a huddle with the youngest and most recently appointed members of her team — the occasionally over-enthusiastic Tom Kidston, and Lucy Magee, the ditsy though very pretty young woman whom Tom had taken to following around the school with slavish devotion.

Mark couldn't make out what Trish was saying but he would have laid odds that it had something to do with how, whenever any money was raised, none of it ever found its way to the English department.

He'd started these daily briefing sessions so that he could get to know his staff better and vice versa. The previous Principal, by all accounts, would barricade himself behind his door on the first day of term and not come out till the term was over, but that wasn't Mark's way at all.

Lola, his wife, believed in the idea of approachability in theory, but not in practice. 'They'll tear you limb from limb,' she'd said, when he'd shared his plans. 'What's the point of having a room of your own if you can't go and hide in it when things get rough?' Lola was a teacher, too, although now she had her hands full looking after their lovely two-year-old twins, Robin and Rosie.

Sometimes he couldn't help thinking that Lola had changed towards him. Before the twins were born he was the centre of her universe. These days he knew he irritated her with his lack of backbone, as she called it. 'For God's sake, Mark, you're the headmaster,' she was always telling him, whenever he confided his latest run-in with one or another member of his staff. 'Just tell them what to do and stop being so understanding of their problems.'

The memory of her words echoed in his ears as he stood in front of the sea of faces, all gazing up at him expectantly. In five minutes' time, the bell would ring for first lesson. He'd better get on with it.

'Next on my list of things to announce is the rather sudden inspection that's been foisted upon us,' he said.

As he'd suspected, the room erupted

in a volcano of moans, groans and vociferous grumbles. Over the din, he attempted to make himself heard. Alexander Drummond had put the book he was marking away and was now doodling on his register, a look of contemptuous indifference on his narrow-jawed face. Lucy Magee was holding her head in her hands dramatically, while Trish Hayman and Tom Kidston jointly did their best to reassure her that really there was nothing at all to worry about. It was going worse than even Mark had expected.

Thankfully, the bell rang and people started to move. Mark raised his hand again — quite ineffectually, however, since everyone was far too exercised about Monday's inspection to pay attention to whatever else he had to add.

'The Inspector's name is Hayden Staples, by the way,' he said. 'I don't know him myself, but some of you may be familiar with it.'

Trish Hayman, who'd stood up quickly at the sound of the bell, stopped whatever it was she was saying to Lucy mid-sentence. At the mention of the Inspector's name, her hand flew to her mouth and the colour suddenly drained from her face as if she'd had a dreadful shock.

From across the room Alexander Drummond's small, round eyes caught hers. Immediately, he averted them. She waved her hand as a signal she needed to talk to him, but either he failed to notice it or he deliberately chose to ignore the gesture. Whichever it was Trish couldn't tell. He headed for the door, no sign of emotion on his face. If ever he played poker, Trish mused, he'd wipe the floor with the other players.

Had she been a couple of stone lighter, Trish Hayman may have managed to slip out through the crowd more easily. But as it was, her exit was a bit of a struggle. Once in the corridor she looked both ways but there was no sign of Alexander Drummond's towering, lean figure among the hordes of youngsters herding themselves in both directions towards their first period.

She cursed Alexander for his evasiveness. What was the matter with the man? Couldn't he see she needed to speak to him? She shouldn't have been surprised, of course. The mere mention of the name Hayden Staples must have sent him into complete shock, for all his deadpan expression. It had certainly had that effect on her — her blood was still pounding and she didn't know how her legs would carry her forward.

Hayden Staples — how dare he come strutting into her school, lording it over her again? 'Don't get yourself worked up,' she told herself. 'You've got your life back on track now and Hayden Staples no longer means a thing.' Stiffening her resolve, she headed for 7B and forty mind-numbing minutes of *The Ancient Mariner*.

Alexander Drummond sat in the biology lab, overseeing Year Eleven as they wrestled with a mock exam he'd thrown at them on the spur of the moment, just so he could have some time alone with his thoughts.

He'd seen Trish Hayman waddling towards him in the staffroom, wearing a look on her face — a mixture of sympathy and pity — that most normal people would reserve for their ancient pet cat as it was about to be put down.

For God's sake, couldn't she leave him alone? What on earth did she imagine she could say that would make him feel any better? Did she think he needed to be reminded that his ex-wife's new husband — the very man who'd cuckolded him — was to be given carte blanche to walk into his classroom without a by-your-leave and pass judgment on his abilities as a teacher? He gripped his red pen with such force that the tip of his thumb and index finger turned white.

It was a mistake to think he'd got over Sandra's betrayal with that smug creep. It had been three years, but he felt just as venomous towards the man now as he had the day Sandra had told him she was leaving him for Hayden Staples. It would take all his self-control, come Monday, not to lay the brute flat out.

* * *

At just after nine the following Monday morning, Hayden Staples drove his brand-new Bentley into the car park of Primrose Park Community College and parked in the only available space, which happened to be the space reserved for the headmaster.

He'd been looking forward to today all weekend, but this morning he'd woken early with cramp in his arm, and the heartburn he'd been complaining of to Sandra only last week had returned, stronger this time, making it impossible to go back to sleep. It had eased slightly as he'd gone about his morning routine, but now he felt grumpy and in need of a strong coffee.

Sandra had sulked when he'd said he didn't feel like joining her on her run this morning, and had done rather a lot of banging about before she'd finally slammed the front door behind her.

From the bedroom window he'd watched her slim, athletic figure Jog down the path and followed her progress until she turned the corner and disappeared from view. He was a very lucky man to have a wife so beautiful and so much younger than himself and to this day he couldn't work out why she'd fallen for him to such an extent that she'd been prepared to leave her husband of only two years.

'I've always preferred older men,' she'd told him and that must have been true because why else would she have fallen for that ancient crock of a man Alexander Drummond, with his love of routine that, according to what Sandra had told him pretty soon after they'd got together, bordered on obsessive.

Meals followed a pattern that couldn't be broken, with fish on Friday and beef on Sunday and porridge, apparently, every morning served at seven-thirty precisely. There was no room in Drummond's life for the spontaneous and that included sex, too, she said. It was the morning Drummond objected to Sandra changing the radio station from Four to One, saying that such a deviation in routine was unheard of in his house, that finally catapulted her into his arms.

Of course, it hadn't all been plain sailing for them. There'd been the small consideration of a wife on Hayden's part, which had entailed much secrecy and deception. But he'd wanted Sandra, from the first moment he'd spotted her on the playing field with a hockey stick grasped firmly between her strong hands, where she'd been enthusiastically coaching the First Eleven.

She'd been at Belvedere Road for less than a week at that time — it was her first job. He was deputy head, dissatisfied with his position and seeing no way of becoming headmaster unless the present head suddenly decided to retire, which was very unlikely, since he'd only been in the job five years and was at least fifteen years away from drawing his teacher's pension. Hayden had needed a change and Sandra had very obligingly provided it.

His marriage to Trish was like most marriages, he supposed. They'd been together for fifteen years and there was nothing left to discover about each other.

Trish couldn't have been more different from Sandra if she'd tried. She'd let herself get fat, for one thing. And she was letting herself get old, with her fussy perms and her dark suits. Worst of all, she was taking him with her. Whenever he caught a glimpse of their joint reflection in the window of the supermarket he couldn't believe that the slim, handsome buck had been replaced by this paunchy, balding old codger. Roundly, he blamed his wife for it.

Sandra became his holy grail and he pursued her with a vengeance. Their passion was finally consummated in the lost property cupboard, where, among unstrung tennis rackets, odd hockey socks and a welter of school scarves and sweaty sweatshirts, they'd sworn their undying devotion to each other.

That had been three years ago. He was a changed man now. A stone lighter, up-to-the-minute in his style of dress — fitter definitely, so Sandra insisted, though some mornings, like today, he wasn't so sure. The struggle to remove his laptop and briefcase from the back seat of the car had brought on another of those hot sweats he'd been experiencing recently. When he'd first begun to complain about them, Sandra had joked he must be going through the menopause. He'd failed to see the humour in her little joke and since then he'd kept his list of ailments to himself. If she suspected he wasn't quite as fit as he was cracked up to be she might start thinking about trading him in for a younger model.

But a glimpse of his reflection in the window of his car told him he was still a good-looking man. On top of all the other changes she'd made in his appearance, Sandra had persuaded him not to go the way of the comb-over, but to get his head shaved quite close. He hadn't liked the look at first — suspecting it might make him look a bit of a thug — but he'd soon got used to it. She'd been right to say that less hair on a man of a certain age often gave the impression of more and in his job looking tough could be seen as a definite advantage.

With the new wife came the new job. After the hoo-ha, when everything came out, neither he nor Sandra could remain at Belvedere Road. Trish, afraid of being humiliated, had applied for Head of English here at Primrose Park. No one

15

had been more surprised than him that she'd actually got the post. But then, Primrose Park had no real cachet. They probably would have given the job to a monkey if it had nodded its head in the right place.

He hadn't seen either Trish or Drummond in the intervening years. 'Was Drummond still eating porridge at seven-thirty every morning?' he wondered. 'And what about Trish? Older, fatter and even more schoolmarmish than ever, no doubt. He was going to get a kick out of observing those two losers in the classroom, that was for sure.'

He noticed a small, nervous man — presumably the Principal — scurrying towards him, hand outstretched and knuckles white with fear. Hayden Staples loved his job. The whites of their eyes, that's what he liked to see.

★ ★ ★

Mark Collins had some apologising to do. It was no use blaming Joe Smith, the caretaker, for the pokiest room in the

16

building — the props room off the drama studio — that had been allocated to the Inspector. To be fair, spare rooms at Primrose Park were at a premium and he'd done well to find one at all.

That's what he'd said to Lola on the phone this morning when she'd rung at eight-thirty — he'd already been in school for an hour by that time doing his best to get to the bottom of his 'to-do' list before Hayden Staples arrived.

'Don't be ridiculous, Mark, that's the caretaker's job,' she'd snapped back. 'You told me yourself he'd promised he'd hunt high and low for suitable accommodation.'

Had he really told her that? It was a lie, of course. Joe Smith had never yet put himself out on his behalf. The most he'd got out of him when he'd made his way over to the caretaker's office after last Friday morning's briefing, during which he'd announced the news of the impending inspection, had been a grudging shrug of the shoulders and some half-hearted words about seeing what he could do.

The whole mess was his fault, really. He was the Principal after all and he should have stayed to help Smith find a room more suitable. Inspectors could be very tetchy if their creature comforts weren't met. There was nothing else for it, he decided — he would just have to grovel. Something he was becoming increasingly skilled at, these days.

Stepping forward, he offered his hand.

'Mr Staples?' he said. 'May I welcome you to our school. I'm Mark Collins.'

★ ★ ★

In the dining room, Tom Kidston spotted Lucy sitting on her own. Wrestling his way past tables, bypassing sports bags and the size twelve boots of lanky year elevens, he finally reached her table. His heart melted at the sight of Lucy's drooping shoulders. He guessed the worst had happened. Her lesson had been inspected and been found wanting.

'Mind if I sit here?'

Lucy flinched as his knee brushed hers beneath the table. She knew it had been a mistake to eat in the canteen. Tom Kidston seemed to have radar when it came to locating her whereabouts, which was fine when she had thirty-two copies of *Pride And Prejudice* to negotiate down two flights of steps, but not at moments like this when all she wanted was to read the paper and wallow in her misery.

THIRD SCHOOL BREAK-IN IN A MONTH, Tom read, upside down. He'd heard about that on the local radio over the weekend. Five new computers had been stolen from Moss Road Primary.

'They should have stored them under lock and key like we're doing with our new gym equipment,' he said, setting down his tray next to Lucy.

'What?'

Her eyes, as she lifted them to his, were red-rimmed. She'd obviously been crying. When she told him just how mean the Inspector had been, listing the areas he felt that she needed to improve on, Tom cursed him roundly.

He'd spotted the man this morning with his skinhead haircut and trousers far too tight for a man of his advancing years, strutting around the school like he owned the place. It was obvious just from looking at him that the man was a thug and a bully. He had a good mind to go round to whichever room it was he was hiding in and punch out his lights for upsetting his girlfriend like that.

Not that Lucy was his girlfriend, exactly. But it was only a matter of time before she realised that the two of them were meant to be. And then, as he carved up his potato and sprinkled it with salt, an idea began to form in his head.

Before lunch Tom had been reading *Le Morte d'Arthur* with Year Twelve. He felt a sudden urge to prove his undying love for Lucy. He had a free period just before afternoon break. If he went to see the Inspector on Lucy's behalf and somehow tried to persuade him to change his report, why, it would be like a knight's quest. And if he managed to change the man's mind, his damsel in distress, eternally grateful, would finally be his.

★　★　★

The usual lackadaisical atmosphere of the staffroom at afternoon break, as staff cheerfully reminded each other that there were only two more periods left before it was time to go home, had been substituted today for one of near frenzy.

Those who hadn't been inspected rushed around making sure they had their lesson plan to hand. Those who had been inspected made things worse for them by recounting their own inspection, in ghastly, grisly detail.

'Been done then have you, Alex?' someone called out above the hubbub.

Alexander Drummond, his eyes fixed firmly on his mug of steaming tea, glowered at Dick Wright, Head of PE, who'd asked the question. Dick was sitting with the rest of the PE staff. They at least could afford to be relaxed for now, since their own inspection wasn't due till next term.

'I doubt I'll be seeing that man in my room today,' Drummond snapped, his jaw clenched.

The PE teachers exchanged wary glances. No one particularly liked Drummond. He always met their banter with looks of complete non-comprehension and most of them had learned to back off years ago. Dick Wright was their departmental head and they owed him loyalty. But there were times — like now — when he allowed his mouth to run away from him.

'You're not thinking of barring him from your room, are you, Alex?' he asked. 'Because that won't get you very far.'

'It's my business what I do inside my own classroom,' muttered Drummond darkly. 'And it's my business, too, who I invite in.'

The PE team went back to their tea. It may have been that Dick Wright, ignoring the 'don't go there, mate' looks that some of his more sensitive colleagues were sending his way, was getting himself ready to remark that, actually, Hayden Staples had the same rights to enter his classroom as the taxman had to knock him up at three in the morning and demand to see his accounts.

But he didn't get the opportunity. For just then the staffroom door burst open. All eyes turned towards Head of Drama, Monica Miller, framed as she was in the doorway, waving her arms frantically and wailing hysterically.

It was a while before everyone paid her much attention. For all anybody in the staffroom knew, this could simply have been a foretaste of the latest Senior Drama Production, which was *Oresteia*, a tragedy that boasted a famous amount of weeping and wailing and gnashing of teeth on the part of the Greek chorus.

She was probably doing it for effect, someone muttered, hoping that the Inspector was there and he'd think this was an example of innovative teaching. Innovative lunacy, someone else muttered, which set off a ripple of tittering that was only silenced when Monica Miller yelled that everyone was to shut up and pay attention at once.

'Something dreadful has happened!' she moaned. 'It's the Inspector. He's dead! I think he's been murdered!'

And then, as was only fitting for someone with her dramatic leanings who cherished nothing more than the full attention of an audience, she fell to the floor in a dead faint.

2

Joe Smith, Primrose Park's caretaker, sat at his desk staring straight ahead and wondering how on earth he was going to get out of this one. Talk about timing. What was that Inspector thinking of, getting himself murdered? Today of all days.

The coppers were here now. Plain clothes. One short and fat, one tall and thin — Laurel and flamin' Hardy. Ten minutes ago, another car had rolled up and this time two women had got out.

'Forensics,' the less snooty one had said, when he'd run outside to ask if he could be of assistance. He'd taken them down to the Props Room, the cubby hole which had been allocated to the Inspector, where the action was, hoping he'd be let in on it. 'How long will you be?' he'd asked them. 'As long as it takes,' they'd said, before thanking him politely and letting themselves inside. It was five o'clock now and, for all anyone knew, they could be there all night.

He'd done everything he could to try to make contact with Big Mick. Phoned his mobile half a dozen times. Texted him with a warning to keep away tonight. He'd even phoned his landline and tried to leave a message with one of his dopey kids. So far none of his calls or texts had been returned and time was running out.

Perhaps there was a chance Big Mick would hear about the murder on the tea-time news and come to the same conclusion he had, which was that it wouldn't be clever of them to try to move two stonking great heavy containers full of brand-new pieces of gym equipment out of the storeroom — the very gear Joe was supposed to be guarding — across the junior playground, then through the back gate into Big Mick's waiting van.

He'd give it one more go, he decided, before he went home for his tea. Punching out Big Mick's digits, he counted the number of times it rang. On the sixth ring Big Mick picked up.

'Thank God,' Joe said. 'Where you been?'

It was nerves that made him speak to Big Mick so sharply. He suspected he'd soon regret it.

'What are you, pal? Me ma?' came the reply.

Joe sniggered to disguise his nerves. Laying on the servility, he apologised for his sharpness, before sharing the news that there'd been a murder, the place was crawling with filth and they were going to have to postpone the job till everything had quietened down.

A reasonable man would have shared Joe's concern that now was not the time to go flaunting stolen goods right under the noses of the local police force. Big Mick, however, had never been a reasonable man and saw no need to start now.

'There's more people involved in this than you and me, pal,' he explained patiently, 'and they're relying on you being where you'd said you'd be at two o'clock tomorrow morning.'

Joe sensed that any objections he made would make not a scrap of difference.

'We'll just have to be even more careful then,' he conceded.

'Right enough, pal,' said Big Mick, affable now he'd re-established just where exactly in the pecking order Joe stood.

★ ★ ★

Mark Collins lay rigid on his side of the bed, anxious not to waken his wife, Lola, who'd had another exhausting day with the twins and needed her precious sleep. The figures on the clock radio glowed one-fifteen. He didn't see how he was ever going to get any sleep tonight after today's events.

'I should be doing something,' he'd said to Lola over dinner — a rather dried-up dinner, actually, but one he hadn't dared complain about, given that amid all the hullabaloo he'd completely forgotten to ring her to let her know how late he was going to be.

'What can you do?' she'd said — rather dismissively, he'd thought. 'It's up to the police now. They won't want you getting under their feet and ruining the evidence.'

Sometimes he wondered if Lola had second sight. How, otherwise, could she have known that he'd been ordered away from the crime scene on not one but three occasions with sharp words from the investigating officer. It was overhearing himself described as 'that meddling headmaster' that had finally sent him scurrying back to his office, from where he'd grabbed his bicycle helmet and headed for home. He'd decided to say no more. One look at Lola's face had told him she'd had enough soul-searching from him for one evening and right now she'd appreciate a bit of peace and quiet while she ate her shepherd's pie.

But the truth was he felt responsible. As headmaster he had an example to set to staff and pupils alike. How was he going to maintain a calm atmosphere with the thought of a murderer on the loose and a body in the props box? Not that the body would be in the props box any longer, of course. But even the thought that it had been was bound to provoke fear and anxiety among children and staff alike. His deputy, Anna Ziegel, for one, had looked like she might faint when the announcement had been made, and someone had said Trish Hayman had been unable to take her last lesson of the day and had had to go home because her poor nerves were shot.

It was no use. He was going to have to get out of bed and drive over to the school. Maybe if he sat in front of the computer screen in his office for long enough, something inspirational that he could read out at tomorrow's assembly would come to him eventually. Anything was better than listening to Lola snoring.

*　*　*

Contrary to the saying that news travels fast, this was not always the case throughout the ranks of the Primrose Park Constabulary. On the contrary, it could take anything up to a week to get round, lurching as it did in fits and starts from one branch of the force to another.

It was for this reason that PCs Booth and Watts, conscientiously patrolling the environs of Primrose Park Community College in their car — a task they'd been engaged in for the past two hours — had heard nothing of the demise of Hayden Staples.

Booth and Watts, far from being primed to keep their eyes skinned on the off-chance of a murderer making a nocturnal reappearance at the scene of the crime, were actually in pursuit of a gang of thieves who, over the past three months, had been responsible for a spate of robberies of valuable equipment from local schools. Regular patrols like this one, according to their Chief Police Officer, were the only way to bring these heartless criminals to Justice.

Neither Booth nor Watts had any confidence that tonight would be the night they caught the thieves. It was Murphy's law, they both agreed, that if they were to ride up and down outside Primrose Park Comp, then the thieves would be happily engaged elsewhere, stealing computers from St Joseph's Primary, for example. But should the coin have landed heads up instead of tails and they'd gone round to St Jo's first, instead of coming over here, then the opposite would have happened.

So it was with disbelief and mounting excitement that, from their secret hiding place behind the garages, they were able to observe the progress of a dirty, white unmarked van, which pulled up outside the school gates, offering them a glimpse of the driver's face as it passed a street lamp.

'Well, well, well,' muttered Booth to a silently watching Watts. 'It's Big Mick and he's heading this way.'

'You think he's doing a job here?' Watts said.

'I'd say so, wouldn't you?'

'I'll call for backup shall I?' Watts suggested nervously.

'No, wait.'

A shadowy figure, his face masked by his hoody, was shuffling across the school-yard in the direction of the now parked van. The policemen watched as, with some difficulty, the man pushed a pallet before him, on which two hefty boxes were stacked.

'An inside job, then,' Watts said. 'I really should call for backup, Boothy. If Big Mick's not taking his medication . . .'

'Good God!'

Watts' sentence was left unfinished as the two policemen, frozen in anticipation, watched dumbstruck as yet another figure — shorter than the first, more slight and wearing glasses — hurled himself across the playground towards the van, from whose driving seat Big Mick was attempting to extricate his not inconsiderable bulk.

With all the fearlessness of a tribal warrior scything the air with a poisoned spear, this third figure waved something resembling a pole of the type that opens windows too high for hands to reach. Gruffly he shouted for the men to stop what they were doing.

'This could be nasty, Boothy,' Watts said. 'I'd really better call for backup.'

'There's no time for that,' Booth snapped, his hand already on the handle of the car door. 'Oh my God, he's hit him!'

At the sound of a cry of pain, the two police officers shot out of the car, reaching the van in seconds. At the sight of the Law, Big Mick did his best to clamber back inside his van and drive off before he could be recognised, but he wasn't quick enough and was smartly hauled back out by the seat of his trousers.

His accomplice lay sprawled on the ground clutching his shoulder and moaning pitifully. His attacker stood over him wielding his window pole authoritatively. The policemen marvelled at his apparent lack of fear. Sometimes, Watts mused, it was as well to be ignorant of the facts — like Big Mick's record for GBH, for example, which would take a speed-reader all morning to get to the end of.

'My name is Mark Collins,' the man said, his voice ringing out clearly in the night. 'This is my school and this — ' he poked the prostrate thief with the tip of the pole — 'is Joe Smith, the school caretaker. Or should I say ex-school caretaker?'

Mark had been buoyed up by a strange sense of exhilaration, which he could only put down to adrenaline. Sitting in his office, staring at a blank computer screen, singularly failing to come up with anything remotely inspirational, sounds from outside had begun to intrude on his train of thought.

This gradual combination of thuds and thumps had finally forced him to get up from his desk, where he'd been sitting in the dark, and move over to the window. He hadn't thought twice about any danger he might be in before dashing outside to give chase.

'All I could think of was the hard work of the PTA and how there was a danger it was all about to go down the drain,' he said to Lola, later, as she sat open-mouthed in admiration and did her best to take in the police officers' words of praise for her husband.

A hero, they'd called him. Her Mark, who flinched at harsh words and had never, in his life previous to tonight, ever laid a finger on a soul!

'I'm so proud of you, darling,' she whispered in his ear, after the police had left and the two of them had gone back to bed, hopefully to snatch another few hours before the twins began their usual clamorous assault on daybreak.

'Oh, it was nothing,' Mark said modestly.

Actually, it took much more bravery on

his part to make his next move. Turning towards Lola, he touched her shoulder with a trembling hand. He half expected to be pushed away — which nowadays was par for the course — but to his surprise Lola leaned her body into his enthusiastically, with no mention of how late — or rather, early — it was. As was the way of all heroes from the beginning of time, he decided to seize the moment, and took her in his manly embrace.

★　★　★

When he arrived on school premises at seven-thirty the following morning, both exhausted and elated after the events of the previous night — not least among them Lola's renewed passion towards him — the police Inspector in charge of the case congratulated him on his night's work.

What a difference a day makes, Mark mused, taking the Inspector's proffered hand. Zero to hero in the space of a few short hours. It was all he could do to concentrate on what the Inspector said as — one of the inner sanctum now, seemingly — he was brought up to speed with progress so far.

They couldn't be certain of the cause of the victim's death until further tests had been carried out, he was told — the results of which were expected later today. But what was clear was that Hayden Staples had suffered a nasty blow to the head and that the murder weapon was probably in the very room in which he'd been murdered.

Mark shivered at the use of the word murdered. It was a stark reminder that this was a real murder being discussed, not something out of Cluedo. All the way to school he'd been planning how to inform his staff of his heroic efforts of the previous night, while still appearing modest and likeable. Now, he felt suddenly ashamed at his self-absorption.

Last night — or rather this morning — in retelling the events to Lola, fact and fiction had sort of blurred and her gasps of admiration, as he piled one detail upon another, had all rather gone to his head. The truth was that if that police car hadn't been patrolling nearby at the exact moment he'd chosen to grab the window-pole and dash outside with it in such a foolhardy manner, then he might be telling a very different story. Worse, someone else might be telling it. It might have been a double murder that was the talk of the staffroom today.

There and then he decided to keep quiet about last night to his staff. If word got out about what he'd done, then all well and good — he'd not deny it. But while there was a murder investigation going on on school premises he intended to concentrate on maintaining morale.

'You might think about turning the children away from the school gates when they start to arrive,' the Police Inspector suggested. 'Once they're inside these gates we'll never be able to contain their imaginative theories. And we can all do without ridiculous rumours reaching the ears of the press, don't you agree, Headmaster?'

Mark could see exactly what the Inspector meant.

'There's already the rumour going round that when the victim was discovered in the props box he was wearing women's clothes, a wig and full make-up,' the Inspector added.

Mark's eyes widened.

'I hadn't heard that,' he said — then, unable to stop himself, 'Was it true?'

The inspector shook his head wearily.

'Pure fiction,' he said.

Mark glanced at his watch.

'I'll get a member of staff posted at the gates right away.' Already it was eight-fifteen and the early birds would be arriving soon. 'Is there any other way I can be of assistance, Inspector, before I go?' he asked.

The Inspector's piercing blue eyes fastened on his own keenly.

'There's the small matter of the murderer, Headmaster,' he said. 'What are your thoughts? Is there anyone among your staff you think might be capable of committing this crime?'

His question, framed so bluntly, took Mark aback. Strangely, this was the first time such a possibility had seriously occurred to him. Hayden Staples' murderer might be sitting in the staff room at this very moment, waiting for him to deliver his morning briefing, and he was going to have to carry on and pretend he wasn't terrified.

★ ★ ★

It was just after twelve-fifteen and Lucy Magee, who had no appetite today, had declined to go with everyone else to the canteen, where the dinner ladies had laid on lunch for the staff who'd bothered to come in today.

This wasn't the first time she'd found herself loitering outside the Principal's office, desperate to offload her burden. The previous night she'd slept in fits and starts, alternately dreaming dreadful dreams and, during long periods of wakefulness, weighing up her options. Should she take the bull by the horns and go to the police straightaway? Or would it be better to speak to Mark first? This morning, when she found herself walking in the direction of Mark's office instead of turning left to go into the staffroom, it was clear that her decision had made itself.

When she'd knocked on his door, she'd been disappointed that Mark hadn't answered. She'd waited a long time, reluctant to go into the staffroom in case he was there. She absolutely couldn't face him right now.

Then Mark had called her name and she'd spun round to see him heading down the corridor towards her. He needed a member of staff to stand outside the school gates, he'd said, to tell the children that there would be no school today.

To Lucy he'd looked different from the way he usually did — which was rather like Harry Potter's older, plumper brother, she'd always thought. Today, he looked like a man beset with serious problems, who needed all the support he could muster. Before she knew it, she'd found herself volunteering for the task.

It had been a relief to leave the overheated building and stand outside in the bracing cold. Groups of children ran over to where she stood, whooping for joy when she told them the news that they could go home, none of them, or so it seemed to her, particularly bothered that yesterday a man had been murdered on school premises. And that somewhere inside this very building a murderer was roaming free.

Standing at the gate, huddling inside her coat and tapping her feet against the cold, she went over Mark's instructions. She'd been told to hang on till nine-fifteen, so as not to miss the stragglers. At nine-twenty, when children were still rolling up, some with anxious or curious parents in tow, she realised she'd missed him at the briefing.

But by now she was feeling better. She decided that holding her tongue might have been a sensible decision. In the middle of the night, the memory of the words Tom had spoken had meant only one thing. But out here, in the late autumn sunshine, she started to wonder if she'd been overreacting.

Her upbeat mood hadn't lasted long, however. Which is why, for the second time today, she'd decided to spill out her

41

suspicions to Mark and let him decide what to do. Once more she recalled those words. 'It's all over, Lucy,' he'd said, creeping up behind her in the staffroom kitchen, so that she'd spilled most of the milk she'd been pouring into her tea on to the worktop. 'There's no need for you to worry about the results of Hayden's observation any more. I've fixed it for you.'

She'd been puzzled and wanted to ask him what he meant, calling out to him above the hubbub, but he'd ignored her and strolled off, looking pleased with himself, and leaving her to work it out for herself. And then Monica Miller had come bursting into the staffroom and delivered her shocking news and all hell had broken out.

Taking a deep breath to quell her mounting nerves, Lucy knocked on the door. This time, to her relief, Mark was in and called her inside.

'The poor girl looks done in,' Mark thought, as Lucy, hovering by his desk, refused the seat he'd offered her.

'My dear girl,' he said, rising from his

chair. 'What's the matter?'

'It's the murderer,' she said, wringing her hands. 'I think I know who it is. I think Tom Kidston killed him and I think I may be to blame.'

3

Tom Kidston wished with all his heart that he hadn't done what he'd done. Prior to yesterday afternoon, he had never broken the law. Not even at university had he committed any of those mandatory student pranks beloved by undergraduates everywhere involving shopping trolleys and traffic cones. He may have borrowed the odd bicycle to get from one lecture to another, but he'd always returned it from where he'd found it, looking over his shoulder in terror as he'd dropped a hastily scribbled apology into the basket.

What on earth had he been thinking of, altering the data on the murdered man's laptop? Thinking of Lucy Magee, clearly, and of how eternally grateful to him she'd be. Except he can't have been thinking straight at the time.

Having spent the previous night and most of this morning scrutinising his behaviour with the newly-acquired, clear-eyed objectivity of a doomed man, he realised that all he deserved from Lucy from now on was contempt.

They'd find his prints on the computer — the murder weapon, so all the staff had just this minute been informed. They'd put two and two together and, wooden-tops that they were, the police would come up with their number-one suspect, none other than himself.

Lucy had dobbed him in already, Tom was convinced. It was obvious from her manner. All morning she'd been avoiding him, leaving rooms as he'd entered them and darting him nervous little looks that she must have thought he wouldn't notice. He'd already worked out that she must be in Mark's office at this very moment, voicing her suspicions, since neither she nor Mark had been present to hear the police officer make his announcement.

It was only a matter of time before the Principal made the short walk from his office to the room the police had taken over. Then it would all be over for him.

Except, Tom reminded himself, grabbing his jacket and heading outside for some air, he was no killer.

A fool, yes, and a perpetrator of an illegal act of fraud. Bad enough in themselves, of course, and he'd be willing enough to put his hand up to the crime. But what if that wasn't enough for the police and they decided they'd already spent enough time looking for a murderer? Why not kill two birds with one stone? He wouldn't be the first honest man to go down for a murder he hadn't committed.

Outside, the cold quickly began to clear his head. He needed to calm down and decide what to do next. A stiff breeze sliced through him as, head down and hands shoved in pockets, he strode the length of the playing field and back again, reliving the events of the previous afternoon.

Yesterday, at lunch-time, when Lucy had told him how badly the Inspector's observation had gone, he'd been furious with Staples for upsetting her so much. He knew she didn't find teaching as easy as he did. Seven years at public school had given him nerves of steel and his experience there meant that nothing any of the kids at Primrose Park could throw at him could ever faze him. Between the ages of seven and eighteen, he'd seen it all.

Lucy was more sensitive than he was. She'd opened up to him once, on a theatre trip, when the large glass of wine he'd bought her during the interval had loosened her tongue.

'It's all right for you, Tom,' she'd said. 'You're a great teacher. The kids love you. But as for me . . . '

At lunch-time yesterday, it was amazing how quickly the idea had wormed its way into his head. He blamed Tennyson and the knights of the Round Table — he'd been reading *Le Morte d'Arthur* just before lunch with his A2s, and had got quite a discussion going on the subject of courtly love.

Everyone agreed — especially the girls — that not enough of it went on these days, and that the world would become a much better place if it did. Why else would he have got it into his thick head that paying a visit to the inspector with the intention of persuading him that he'd been quite wrong about Lucy was a good idea?

The door of the props room, which had been loaned to the inspector as his office, had been closed, but after he'd knocked a couple of times and no one answered, he'd decided he wasn't going to let that stand in his way. Staples looked the type to ignore the usual courtesies, with his skinhead haircut and his too-tight trousers. He was probably in there all right, Tom decided, but he just couldn't be bothered answering. Well, two could play at that game.

Cautiously, Tom had opened the door and stuck his head round it. 'Oh, I thought I heard you say come in,' he'd already decided to say, should Staples have been there after all. But the room was empty.

Tom resolved to wait inside. Probably the man had gone to answer a call of nature, so he wouldn't be long, he decided. To kill time, he wandered over to the desk. There was the Inspector's laptop — a shiny, state-of-the-art, top-end-of-the-market model that Tom had long lusted after himself but, on his salary, would never be able to afford.

He'd only intended to have a little look at it — to see for himself if it really did all those fancy things it was advertised as being able to do. But, on lifting the lid, his attention was caught by a file bearing the familiar name, Primrose Park. Without a second thought, he opened it. Scrolling down the page, Lucy's name jumped out at him and, unable to stop himself, his eyes flicked over the words.

What Staples had written about Lucy was intolerable. *Unprepared, unaware of differing learning styles, exhibiting a lack of clarity in her approach to her class,* and that was just for starters. The jargon went on and on. If Lucy saw this she'd be devastated, Tom realised. Worse, if Mark Collins saw it he'd use it as an excuse to get rid of her once her probationary year was over in a few months' time. And where would Tom be then? He might as well give up teaching himself!

In that moment, all that was driving him was an urgent impulse to make things better. He'd felt perfectly justified in altering a sentence here, a phrase there, and now and then deleting a negative word and replacing it with one that was much more positive. Boldly running his fingers over the keys had empowered him. Smiling, he pressed save, closed the lid and replaced the laptop on the desk.

He'd been so involved in creating a new report for Lucy that he'd forgotten about Staples altogether, but the sudden and unexpected clamour of the bell and the clatter of feet accompanied by the raised voices of the children as they began to make their way around the school again, brought him out of his trance and into the realisation that he'd just tampered with the inspector's report — a legal document — and that once Staples returned and read it through again, he'd realise that what was on the screen wasn't what he'd written.

How on earth could he put right what he'd done? Tom broke out in a cold sweat, as it dawned on him that it would be impossible now to change the report back to its original state. The only thing left for him to do was to get out of this room right away and put as much space between it and him as possible.

So that was what he'd done. Making his way to his form room, he'd calmly taken the register and then gone off to teach. The one thing that might save him, he decided, as he took his classes on automatic pilot, was that the Inspector was pushed for time. Why would he bother re-reading what he'd written in the morning, when he had so many other members of staff to visit? With a bit of luck, Tom convinced himself, he'd simply print out his report and stick it in one of those manila files he'd seen cluttering his desk. Then it would be farewell, Primrose Park, and see you in another three years.

By the time break had arrived, he'd convinced himself that his plan was much more likely to succeed than fall, which was why he'd cheerfully told Lucy that she needn't worry about her observation report any longer.

Now Staples was dead, Tom's finger-prints were all over the murder weapon and Lucy, far from showing her gratitude to him was keeping as far away from him as possible, clearly convinced he was a murderer. Fear, like a clammy hand, closed round his heart and squeezed it tight. He racked his brains to recall his actual words. What if he'd said not, 'I've fixed things for you,' but, 'I've fixed Staples for you.' There was a world of difference between the two.

All he'd ever wanted was for Lucy to love him. But she could never love a murderer. In the middle of the playing field, Tom stood stock still. Might she find it in her heart to love a man who was brave enough to confess to a lesser crime, even though now that Staples was dead there was no way it could ever be discovered? He would go at once to see the Principal, and throw himself on his and Lucy's mercy.

* * *

'Hit on the back of a head with a laptop,' Dick Wright, the head of PE, declared. 'Poor man. At least he wouldn't have seen it coming.'

Some of the members of staff sat at a

table in the staffroom, listlessly nursing mugs of tea. There was plenty to do — books to mark, paperwork to catch up on, lessons to plan. But no one felt like doing any of these things. All any of them wanted to do was talk about the murder.

'Who do you think did it, then?' Dick Wright said, to no one in particular.

'Do you think we should be discussing that?' Anna Ziegel said disapprovingly.

'Well, there's nothing else to talk about,' Dick Wright replied.

'On the contrary,' Anna said. 'What about the headmaster apprehending Joe Smith, just as he was about to make off with the new gym equipment?'

Mark had briefly been a hero when he'd stopped the school caretaker and his thieving cohorts from pinching the proceeds of the PTA's latest fund-raising effort. There were exclamations of astonishment and calls for the whole story to be told immediately from all around the table. Anna was all too willing to oblige, now that she had everyone's attention. As Deputy Principal, she felt she had a responsibility to do something about the gloomy mood that had settled on the staffroom since the events of yesterday, and was happy that with this piece of news she'd managed to turn the mood around so quickly and completely.

'You wouldn't think he had it in him, would you?' Dick Wright said with grudging admiration, after he'd heard the whole story. 'A whippersnapper like that.'

'Brains will always win out over brawn, you know,' Anna replied, with a smile that didn't quite reach her eyes.

Dick Wright was more than six foot tall and built like a brick wall. A titter of appreciation passed around the table like a Mexican wave. For one short moment, it seemed as if Hayden Staples' murder had been forgotten.

★ ★ ★

Mark Collins listened aghast to Lucy Magee's accusations against Tom Kidston, not knowing what to make of them. Lucy thought Tom had murdered Staples and that he'd done it for her. He'd certainly got hold of the wrong end of the stick when he'd thought that both Tom and Lucy were exhibiting the first telltale signs of a burgeoning romance. It was an easy mistake to make since they were often together. But Lucy soon put him right.

'No, no,' she said. 'It's not like that at all. At least not on my part.'

Tom had monopolised her from the very first day she'd joined the school, she told him, as she perched on the edge of her seat in his office. At first she'd been grateful for his help. Primrose Park was a sprawling building on two sites and she'd never have learned to find her way around if Tom hadn't taken her under his wing. But as she began to find her way about more easily, it began to irritate her that everywhere she turned there he was, gazing after her with those moonstruck eyes of his.

His obsession with her had taken a stronger turn on a theatre trip just before half-term, she went on to say. They'd taken Year Nine to see *Blood Brothers* and, during the interval, she and Tom had shared a drink together.

'I think I may have rather given the impression that I needed looking after. Or rather, that I needed looking after by him.'

She bit her bottom lip in — Mark thought — a very attractive way. It was no wonder Tom was besotted by her. Everything about her appearance ticked all the right boxes and on top of that there was a sweetness about her — an air of vulnerability that very few women seemed to want to exhibit in this modern day and age.

His wife, Lola, for one, wouldn't know how to spell vulnerability let alone admit to being vulnerable herself. She was more the earth-mother type. Fierce and protective of her brood — their adorable twins — and capable of murder should anyone try to harm any of the people she loved best.

Murder. The word brought him back to Lucy's shocking accusation. Was Tom Kidston really capable of squaring up to another man and assaulting him — delivering a death blow — just because that man had upset the woman he loved?

Mark rose from his chair and crossed to the window, hoping that by staring out of it for long enough an answer to what he should do next might fall from the sky. Men had killed for women since time immemorial. But Tom Kidston? He was a boy, not a man, still wet behind the ears. He was startled by a sharp rapping on the door.

'Come in,' he croaked weakly, from his place by the window.

As the handle turned he felt the rush of air as someone entered. Lucy gave a cry of fear and when he spun round, her face was white with shock.

'Sir.' It was Tom Kidston. 'I've got a confession to make.'

★ ★ ★

It was a relief to have this snatched couple of hours at home with Lola. He felt calmer just for having offloaded his dilemma on to her. Should he report Tom Kidston to the police for fraud or should he cover for him?

'The thing is,' he said, over a much-needed ham sandwich, 'his prints will be all over that computer. I'm surprised they haven't questioned him already.'

Lola poured him more tea. Mark's appearance at this time of the afternoon was as welcome as it was unusual. The twins were in the middle of their regular afternoon nap and she was bored. Sometimes she felt guilty that motherhood wasn't quite enough for her and, although she'd never said as much to Mark, there were occasions when she sincerely regretted giving up her teaching post after her maternity leave had run out, citing as an excuse not one but two babies to look after and no family nearby to help.

Mark waited for her to speak, but she remained silent. In Mark's experience that meant only one thing. She knew what she'd do in the circumstances, but she suspected it was something he wouldn't feel comfortable with himself.

'You think I should report him, don't you?' He took his refilled cup from her hand.

'I think you've already made up your mind not to,' she said, with a patient smile. 'You've just spent the last twenty minutes praising Tom Kidston's teaching ability to the skies and putting the whole sorry business down to the folly of love.'

Mark wrinkled his brow.

'Have I really?' he said.

'You know you have.' Lola grinned. 'You big old softy.'

'If you could only have seen how remorseful he was,' he said mournfully.

Lola crossed to where he slouched, exhausted, in his chair and planted a tender kiss on his brow. It mortified her that only a few days ago she'd accused him of having no backbone.

Well, he'd shown plenty of backbone when he'd single-handedly taken on those thieves and he was showing it now, only in a different way. Sensitive men like Mark were thin on the ground and rarely appreciated in the macho world of work. She was lucky enough to have found one and from now on she was going to make sure she appreciated it.

But there was the tricky subject of

Lucy's bad report, before Tom had nobbled it. Sooner or later Mark was going to have to decide what to do about her.

'I was wondering,' he said, putting down his empty plate and stretching his legs. 'Do you think it would be in bad taste to take flowers over to Staples' widow?'

'I think it's a lovely idea,' she said. 'If you like, I'll get Susie next door to babysit for an hour and I'll come along with you.'

★ ★ ★

Sandra Staples cowered behind her front door, her dressing-gown pulled tightly around her. Surely he wouldn't have the nerve to come round here after the way she'd dismissed him on the phone? The first three times she'd made the mistake of answering. But since his last call, she'd simply ignored it and let the machine pick up the message.

'I only want to say I'm sorry,' he'd kept on saying. 'I know you think I hated him but I never meant for this to happen.'

What did he mean by that? Surely, he could only mean one thing, too terrible to contemplate. She should have threatened him with the police right away. Now he was here, ringing her doorbell till she let him in. And then what? She was five feet two in her stockinged feet and Alexander was a giant. She stood no chance.

'Go away,' she yelled through the letter-box with a courage she didn't feel. 'I don't want you round here!'

A woman's voice called back at her.

'Mrs Staples. My name's Lola Collins. I'm here with my husband, Mark, headmaster at Primrose Park. We've come to offer our condolences,' the woman said.

Once more, Sandra's phone clamoured into life, stretching her nerves even tighter. Throwing herself against the door, she unbolted it and, grabbing Lola's arm, she pulled her in. Mark, who'd been holding Lola's hand, stumbled in behind her, accidentally decapitating three of the stems they'd stopped off en route to buy.

'Do you want to answer that?' Lola nodded in the direction of the phone.

61

She thought that Sandra looked tired and drawn, which was understandable considering the circumstances in which she'd lost her husband. But there was something else. She appeared frightened too, flinching with every shrill ring of the telephone.

'No, I don't.' Her voice rang out, more shrill even than the phone. 'I know who it is and I don't want to speak to him. It's my ex-husband, if you want to know. His name's Alex Drummond — you must know him, he's been on your staff for about a hundred years.'

She addressed the last part of her remark to Mark, who stared back at her openmouthed. How on earth could droopy old Alex Drummond ever have been married to this sultry-looking female?

'He's been hounding me all day and I'm frightened he might come round here and try to do something!'

The pitch of Sandra's voice was getting higher, verging on the hysterical, inducing in Mark a feeling of alarm.

'What do you mean?' he asked.

'I mean he's a man who bears a

grudge,' Sandra said. 'When I left him for Hayden, he threatened to kill both of us. Well, Hayden's been found dead at Alexander's place of work and now I'm afraid he might be coming for me, just in case I've rumbled him.'

4

'What if I make us all a nice cup of tea?' Lola led Sandra Staples, her face streaked with mascara-stained tears, over to the settee. She flopped down into it, like a rag doll and, distraught, buried her face in her hands through which a stream of garbled words escaped. Mark made out 'murderer', 'me next', and 'complete and utter nutter', bubbling up through the tears. In desperation, he sought reassurance from Lola's eyes.

Grieving widows, who were terrified their ex-husbands were about to bump them off after they'd already done away with their arch rival, weren't something he'd ever found himself dealing with before in the course of his career as a headmaster, and he rather thought a woman — any woman — would handle it better than himself.

Unfortunately, there was no reassurance to be found in Lola's uncharitable eyes. Instead, she tilted her head towards the door, grabbed hold of his wrist and almost dragged him into the kitchen behind her. He opened his mouth to complain at such rough treatment but, with a finger to her lips, she shot him a warning look.

In the kitchen, empty wine bottles cluttered every surface and the sink was laden with dirty glasses, which — once she'd filled the kettle and put it on — Lola began to attack with hot, soapy water.

'The woman's clearly drunk,' she hissed at Mark. 'Look at the state of this kitchen! And there are at least two empty half bottles of vodka in the living room. Did you notice?'

Mark hadn't, not having Lola's gimlet eyes. He thought it was rather harsh of her to be so judgmental towards a woman whose husband had just been murdered and said so. If he was ever to be murdered, God forbid, he hoped she'd get blind drunk and not stop crying for a week, he said.

'I'm not being judgmental!' Lola

protested. 'All I'm saying is that people often distort the truth when they've had a bit too much alcohol.'

Mark pondered this.

'Are you saying she's just making it up about Alexander threatening to kill Staples?'

'Not that bit, so much. That bit I can believe,' Lola said. 'I'd threaten to kill you if I thought you were having an affair.'

'I wouldn't dare.' Mark rubbed his sore wrist.

Lola's sharp eyes scoured the kitchen for the wherewithal to dry the glasses, finally alighting on a grubby tea-towel hanging over the back of a chair. She flung it at him with orders to dry.

'What I mean is that threatening and doing are two completely different things,' she said. 'Yes, poor, broken-hearted cuckold that he was, he threatened to kill them when he learned of their affair. No, he didn't actually carry out his threat. And if you ask me it's just as unlikely that he's on his way here to kill his ex-wife.'

Lola might be right, Mark conceded. If Alexander had been plotting the downfall of Hayden Staples for so long, then surely he could have thought of something a bit more imaginative than banging him on the back of the head with a laptop computer? He was Head of Science, for goodness' sake. Surely a nice little explosion or some electronic wizardry would have been more up his street?

'She probably thinks that Drummond wants her dead because deep down she thinks she deserves it for ruining his life,' Lola said. 'Which is nonsense, of course — just the booze talking. The woman is clearly a drama queen who just likes being the centre of attention.'

It never ceased to amaze Mark how dismissive women could be of other women.

'Whatever happened to the sisterhood?' he said, flicking the tea-towel playfully across her behind.

Lola laughed and flicked soapsuds back at Mark, who darted towards her and pinned her to the sink, holding down both her arms, to stop her doing it again, whereupon she squealed in mock terror. It was in the midst of this horseplay that, gradually, they both became aware of

Sandra Staples' presence in the doorway, her haphazardly fastened dressing-gown now showing rather more leg and cleavage even than previously.

'Sorry to interrupt you,' she smirked, 'but I thought you should know that even if you two think I'm off my rocker, the police don't. I've just rung them and they're on their way round to speak to me about my suspicions right now.'

Mark and Lola gaped at her, embarrassed not only for being caught messing about like two teenagers, but also because she'd overheard them discussing whether or not their hostess was a drunk who wasn't quite right in the head. All this when she'd so recently been bereaved, too.

'So if you don't mind, I'd rather you two made yourselves scarce,' she added. 'I'm sure you both have plenty to do.'

★ ★ ★

They drove back home feeling rather subdued. They'd agreed that Mark should drop Lola off and then pop back to school to see if there were any further developments. He was desperate to know when he could reopen the school — something only the Detective Inspector running the investigation would be able to tell him, and he was also curious to find out if Alexander Drummond had been taken in for questioning.

It was five o'clock by the time he'd dropped Lola off at home. Drummond, a conscientious member of staff, never left his desk until five-thirty at the earliest. If he wasn't there when Mark got to school, then he'd know that they were taking Sandra Staples' suspicions seriously.

On the drive home, he'd given Lola's theory a great deal of consideration. She hadn't taken to Sandra Staples, that much was obvious, and frankly, neither had he. But not enough to dismiss her as a hysterical and unreliable drunk, as Lola had.

Drummond had been teaching at Primrose Park since time immemorial. He'd never taught anywhere else, as far as Mark was aware. But who, among his staff, himself included, knew anything about him really? The fact that he'd been married at all certainly wasn't common knowledge, let alone the fact that the woman he'd married had run off with the man who'd been found dead on school premises!

When Lola had put forward her theory — that if Drummond had intended murdering Staples and then his ex, he'd have done it as soon as he'd discovered that their affair wasn't just a fling but something that spelled the end of his marriage — she'd failed to take into account one very important fact.

Alexander Drummond was not a spontaneous man. He was noted for his slavish devotion to routine, his lessons never deviated from his scheme of work and he arrived at the same time every day, leaving at the same time, too. In Mark's opinion — and probably in the opinion of everyone else who taught at Primrose Park — Drummond was a thinker not a doer.

He'd had three long years to think about how to kill his enemy. The perfect opportunity had presented itself out of the blue, and Drummond, clever enough to realise that no one would ever suspect him of getting even in such a clodhopping manner as to deliver a blow to the head with a laptop, had killed Staples in that exact same way. A brilliant double bluff, Mark decided.

★　★　★

A fuming Alexander Drummond flung open the door of the interview room at the police station, where he'd been brought by police car two hours earlier. He strode the length of the building trying to find a way out, before remembering he needed a taxi to get him back to school and his mobile phone was still sitting on his desk. Still fuming, he headed back to the desk to demand that the officer on duty make the call to the taxi firm for him. It was the least they could do after the way he'd been treated.

He'd been marking the test he'd given his Year Elevens yesterday — before all this business with Staples had blown up, and lamenting the woeful standard of the answers — when a uniformed officer had hauled him out of his room and down here to the station with some ridiculous accusation that the police were starting to think he knew more about the death of Hayden Staples than he was letting on.

They'd made him wait in a windowless room for an hour with no refreshment while they'd waited for the duty solicitor to turn up. Then, when the man finally arrived and Alexander had put him straight about what a load of nonsense all this was, he'd been forced to wait yet another half an hour for the arrival of whoever was meant to be interviewing him.

The cheek of it, he'd railed at the solicitor while they'd waited, an irritating little man in Alexander's opinion, who kept on telling him how much better it would be for him if he co-operated.

'I know all about innocent men being locked up for life for co-operating,' he'd snapped back, 'and if you imagine for a moment that I intend making the police's job any easier, then you have another thing coming.'

Of course, he'd been able to give them chapter and verse about his movements on the day of the murder, and they'd had no option but to release him — rather reluctantly in his opinion. Now they were going to have to start their enquiries all over again.

He leaned back in the taxi that was taking him back to school, feeling smug at this prospect. The police could be so stupid at times, he thought — probably only about half a dozen GCSEs between them if the lot he'd had to deal with were anything to go by.

'Thanks for your co-operation,' they'd said, as they'd let him go. Ha! There were things he knew that would solve their crime for them in minutes. But they'd get no help from him. Not after this humiliation. His connection with Staples would be all over the staffroom tomorrow and once again there'd be tongues wagging and fingers pointing his way. He might as well write an announcement on the staffroom whiteboard.

For your information, the murdered man stole my wife and made a fool out of me.

Not content with mocking him in life, Staples had succeeded in making a fool of him from beyond the grave.

★ ★ ★

Back in his office, Mark did his best to get on with some work, but he couldn't concentrate. Staff appraisals were coming up soon — the first he'd ever done at this school — and he wasn't particularly looking forward to the task. He had Lucy Magee to deal with, for one thing. Picking up her file, he leafed through it. Could he really justify keeping her on after that dreadful observation she'd had?

He sighed. Everything always came back to Hayden Staples in the end, however hard he tried to divert himself. He decided it might be less upsetting to concentrate on someone a bit less flaky and his eyes alighted on Trish Hayman's file.

Poor Trish had been really turned over by the events of the previous day. She'd run out of her classroom during period nine, according to Kylie Simms who'd come knocking on his door asking what they were all supposed to do now.

He'd sent his deputy in to the ladies' cloakroom after her to check on her. Shortly afterwards she'd gone home and hadn't been in since. He really must give her a ring and find out if she was feeling up to coming in tomorrow. How long would it be before his school was back to running normally? he wondered. And would they ever be able to use the props room again?

There he was again, mulling over that dreadful deed. Concentrate, Collins, he told himself, applying himself to the data on the page. It was a bit of a surprise to discover from her file that Trish Hayman had only been with them three years. He'd always thought of her as being one of the old-timers, like Drummond.

Her last school had been Belvedere Road, he read. He shifted in his seat. Wasn't it Belvedere Road where the Stapleses had met and fallen in love? So Sandra Staples had confided, presumably while the vodka was still kicking in, and before she'd turned nasty and thrown them out.

As his eyes scanned over these pages, he'd never had the need to read before, more snippets of information jumped out at him, making him feel very uncomfortable indeed. Here was Trish's application letter for the post of Head of English at Primrose Park.

This was interesting — she'd written that she'd been happy in her role as second in the English department at Belvedere Road and would be there now, were it not for the breakdown of her marriage, which had made it impossible for her to remain working in the same establishment as her soon-to-be-ex-husband and his new girlfriend.

The previous Headmaster had scribbled something in the margin. Mark screwed up his eyes behind his glasses to make it out: *Admire her honesty!!!* he read. Her letter of application was signed *Trish Staples*.

The sound of someone tapping on his door brought him out of his shock. Alexander Drummond, wearing his usual deadpan expression, stuck his head round the door. Mark, in the grip of a cold sweat, could barely find the voice to say hello, but he managed to find the strength to lift up Trish's file and wave it in Drummond's direction.

'Trish Hayman,' he croaked.

Drummond curled his lip in imitation of a smile.

'I'll say that for ye,' he said. 'You've more brains than that policeman who's just had me down the station for two hours.'

'Why didn't you say anything before?'

Drummond shrugged.

'Not my job. She may be a bit of an old bat, but I don't want to be the one responsible for waving her dirty linen all over the media,' he said. 'Are you going to tell the police?'

Mark knew it wasn't a matter of if but when. What if he went round there? Told her he was just calling to see how she was. Asked her if there was anything she wanted to tell him. Remind her that sometimes we all felt better for getting things off our chest.

He started to pick up the jumble of files on his desk in an attempt to restore a bit of order to it. A note, scribbled on a piece of paper headed with the logo of Primrose Park Constabulary, fluttered to the floor, and he knelt to retrieve it. This must have been put on his desk when he'd been at home with Lola, before they'd decided to take flowers to Mrs Staples. The second Mrs Staples, as he should perhaps think of her now.

'Good news?' Drummond said, noticing some of the tension drain from Mark's face as he read the note.

Mark slipped the note into his pocket. He hoped sincerely that it was — but he had no intentions of sharing it with Drummond.

'I've a few things to do here before I go home, Alexander,' he said. 'So if you don't mind I'm going to have to kick you out of my office.'

Drummond let himself out without demur. Mark leaned back in his chair, triumphantly resting his arms behind his head for a moment. If Lola were here now she'd be giving him a round of applause.

★　★　★

Idiotic as it might seem, given that Trish must have known why he was here, she positively welcomed him inside with open arms.

'When you live on your own, as I do,' she said, rushing off to make a cup of tea he didn't really want, 'it's quite possible to go from Friday afternoon to Monday morning without seeing a soul.'

Mark made noises of sympathy but she brushed them away.

'I was toying with the idea of getting a kitten only last week,' she said. 'For the company, you know. Kylie Simms' cat had just had a litter and she was going round asking everyone in the class if they wanted one.'

She handed him a mug which bore the words *I'm only teaching until my novel's published*, adding wryly that in the circumstances she'd made the right decision when she'd decided not to, since a prison sentence would mean there'd be no one to look after it.

'It's not going to be as long a stretch as you think, you know, Trish,' Mark said, fishing the note, whose contents he'd concealed from Drummond, from his jacket pocket and handing it to her.

Her eyes lit up when she read the words and her strained face relaxed into a smile.

'*Cause of death — heart attack*,' she read. 'It says here that the blow to the head may have caused him to lose balance, but it couldn't possibly have killed him!'

But her delight at what she'd read was short-lived.

'But dragging him over to the props chest and hiding his body inside,' she said. 'That won't look good.'

Mark agreed.

'Why did you do it, Trish?' he asked her gently.

'What? Bash him? Or hide him in the props box?'

'Both, really.'

'Simple,' she said. 'I bashed him because, once again, he'd humiliated me. And I put him inside that box in order to humiliate him back. Hayden always dreaded looking undignified, you see.'

It was Saturday afternoon and Mark

was doing a stint of twin-sitting. Lola, who'd just come home from the super-market, dropped a paper into his lap.

'*Super-head goes to the top of the class,*' she read. '*Headmaster Mark Collins foils burglary and clears up the mystery of the death of school inspector.*'

Mark flung the newspaper on to the floor with a groan. Since Trish had been arrested and her story, alongside the story of the attempted burglary, had come out, he'd been pursued by the Press day and night, and was getting heartily sick of his fifteen minutes of fame.

'Poor you,' Lola said, dropping a kiss on his head.

Mark was modesty personified and she loved him for it.

'Poor Trish,' he said. 'Locked up in prison with God knows what kind of people.'

'Criminals, you mean?'

She picked up the newspaper from the floor and smoothed it with her hands, a proud smile on her face.

'Don't worry,' she added. 'She'll be out of the slammer in no time.'

He sincerely hoped she was right. For Trish's own sake she was going to have to share with the jury a great many of the belittling insults Staples had hurled at her, the day she'd gone to see him in the props room to plead with him to stay out of her classroom and out of her life. It wasn't going to be easy for her to repeat even half the dreadful things he'd said to her.

'If only he hadn't turned his back on me just as he was saying he couldn't wait to see if I was as boring in the classroom as I'd been in bed,' she'd told him, as the police led her away. To his mind, she deserved a fair hearing and a great deal of compassion and he prayed with all his heart she'd get it.

Lola went into the kitchen to unpack the shopping.

'You're going to be short of an English teacher,' she called out to him.

Up until a couple of hours ago he'd thought he was going to be short of two. But he'd decided to give Lucy Magee a second chance. He certainly wasn't going to have Staples dictating to him from beyond the grave after the way he'd treated Trish Hayman. It suddenly occurred to him that Lola was sounding him out about Trish's job. Well, why not? She'd been a Head of English before the twins had arrived — and a damn fine one at that.

'I wouldn't want to do it full-time. A job share might be good, though.'

Actually, that wasn't such a bad idea, Mark thought. Progressive. He'd just have to find someone else to share the post. He'd get on with wording the advert right away.

'You do realise you'll have to apply just like everyone else?' he called out.

Lola appeared in the doorway, holding a box of cereal.

'Do I look bovvered?' she said challengingly.

Mark grinned at her, relieved that life was getting back to normal at last.

Looking After Jopo

1

The girl in front of me looked so pathetic, so hopeful and so desperately young — like she'd raided her mum's make-up bag and gone overboard with the eyeshadow — that it would have been cruel to say no to her request. I was just playing for time.

'I'll make sure he's in his jimjams before I take off. And I'll leave you loads of mags. And biscuits. You won't be bored! Promise!'

So even Sharon had me down as a saddo with no life, assuming I'd be in all evening with no exciting plans of my own. So far, so right. I leaned against my doorframe, leisurely picking at some flaking paint, doing my best to look like I was someone mentally going through their diary. It should have been me standing where she was, dressed in high heels and a skirt up to there, clutching my mobile phone in certain anticipation that any minute now I'd get a text.

Sharon was barely eighteen, for goodness' sake. I was pushing thirty. Yet she was asking me to baby-sit for her!

'You won't be back too late, will you? Only I've got work tomorrow,' I said.

I had work every day, except Sunday. Seven-thirty am to six in the evening at Corrigan's Café, serving breakfast, lunch and day-long snacks to the residents of the Robinwood Estate and the occasional passing trade.

Sharon's pixie face gleamed earnestly.

'Oh no! I'm only going out for a drink with a few of the girls,' she insisted.

'Not clubbing, then?'

People have told me I have a suspicious nature. I wouldn't deny that, but then I remind them there are mitigating circumstances. My mother, in other words. She's enough to affect anyone's personality.

'Not clubbing! No way! Not on a Monday. Place is full of students!'

I remembered a line from that *Othello* play we'd done at school. Methinks the lady doth protest too much. I didn't trust Sharon. She was too jumpy, too gushing and, besides, she was already dressed to kill.

My instinct told me to say no. But then I thought of little Joseph — or Jopo, as everybody called him. If I refused to go over the road and baby-sit, would she just go out anyway and leave him sleeping in his bed? I didn't think she was the type who would, but then how well did I really know her?

She'd moved in a couple of weeks ago, and since then we'd said hello a few times. The other Sunday, a friend of hers had turned up, beeping the horn of a rusty old saloon till a sleep-bedraggled Sharon had finally opened the door to admit her. Sharon had run across half an hour later to beg me to take Jopo for an hour so her friend could take her shopping to the out-of-town hypermarket. Since she kindly offered to do a bit of shopping for me as a thank you, I readily agreed.

Jopo had proved to be an angel child — sunny-natured and resourceful, no trouble at all. Actually, I'd quite fallen in love with him. I'd said, 'Any time,' when she'd thanked me as we'd said goodbye, so whose fault was it that I was the first person she'd called on tonight?

'Oh, go on then,' I said. 'Give me half an hour and I'll be round.'

Sharon's face broke into a wide smile. 'Cheers, Cate! You're mint!'

'I know,' I said, regretting it already.

I was regretting it even more at ten o'clock when, reclining on Sharon's flimsy settee, and having yawned my way through yet one more episode of Britney's love life by way of Jordan's exercise routine, my reverie was disturbed by a hammering at the door.

I leapt up, heart thudding. It didn't sound like your typical friendly neighbour knock. The one where someone drops by to borrow a few slices of bread till the morning.

It was late at night. I was on my own. There was an eighteen-month-old baby upstairs, sleeping like — well, a baby — and this was the Robinwood Estate. Known locally as the Robbing Wood Estate. Although, to be fair, I didn't put this intruder into that category. No one was going to knock on your door if they were about to steal your telly, were they?

'I'm not opening this door till you tell me who you are and what you want! There's a child sleeping upstairs!'

I sounded pretty impressive, even to my own ears, but my insides were churning.

'I want what you owe me, that's all! Hand it over and I'll go. Muck me about and there'll be trouble.'

Suspicious thoughts pressed down on me. I'd had Sharon down as a nice girl. Not all that bright — but she wasn't the only girl on this estate to opt for a qualification in motherhood instead of her GCSEs. But this was not nice, leaving me literally holding the baby and swanning off like that just so she could dodge her debt collector.

'She's not in!' I yelled. 'Come back tomorrow!'

'Open this door!'

Another few kicks and a dozen obscenities. I blame the decline in reading standards for the paucity of some people's vocabulary.

I decided to comply with his request. I opened up.

'Who the hell are you?'

It crossed my mind to reply that it should have been me posing that question — but only very briefly. He was only my height — which is five feet six — but he looked nasty with it, the type who'd have a chip on his shoulder for being short. I couldn't see much of his face, it being dark and him wearing the ubiquitous baseball cap and hoody.

'I'm the babysitter,' I said. 'If you want Sharon you're going to have to try later.'

He looked stumped. I stared him out, wondering what he made of me.

'Do you want me to give her a message?'

He thrust his hands into his jeans pockets.

'Tell her I'll be back.'

He spoke with menace in his voice, pushing his face into mine as he did so. The stench of stale beer assailed my nostrils. It was a cold night but I began to prickle with sweat. It was a relief when he turned to go.

'Tell her she'd better be in tomorrow,' he called out over his shoulder, as he slouched away into the night.

Before he changed his mind and decided to invite himself inside, I shut the door firmly and shot the bolt. Feeling drained of all energy, I flopped back down on the settee. The whole scene had played out in less than ten minutes but it had felt like a lifetime.

I was in desperate need of a cup of tea to steady my nerves, but was shaking so much that I didn't think my legs would carry me to the kitchen. Far better, I decided, to lie down on Sharon's settee, close my eyes for a few minutes and wait for my heart-rate to slow down.

★   ★   ★

When I woke up, a murky light was creeping through a chink in the curtains. It took me a moment to realise where I was. What was I doing here on Sharon's grimy settee when I should be in my own bed tucked up under sweet-smelling sheets? And, more urgently, where on earth was Sharon?

The sound of someone moving about

began to register in the dark recesses of my brain. Not footsteps, no, but a swish-bump-swish-thump sort of sound, like someone practising a new dance routine over and over again. Was it Sharon, still high after too many alcopops, prancing about in the privacy of her bedroom? I called her name, but there was no reply. I was stiff from having lain on that cramped little sofa all night so it took me a while to haul myself upright. The swish-bump-swish-thump was getting nearer. When the handle of the living room door began to turn, I froze.

'Jopo want dink!'

Relief flooded through me. I stuck my head round the settee and grinned at him foolishly. Hiding behind the settee was probably something he did himself on a regular basis. When he saw me he just smiled that smile of his that lit up not only his face, but the whole room with it.

'Hi, Jopo,' I said. 'Remember me?'

Well, what else was I expected to say? Dusting myself off — did Sharon even possess a vacuum cleaner, let alone know what one was for? I struggled to my feet.

'Where Mummy?'

Wouldn't we all have liked to know the answer to that one? I made a mental note to myself. Next time my instinct told me something, go with it.

Meanwhile, I had one very damp and very hungry toddler to sort out. Fortunately, Jopo was an obliging host. He knew where his changing mat was and all the bits and pieces that went with it. But I can only say that if this had been the Eurovision Nappy Changing Competition I would have scored *nul points*. I might even have been booed off. But Jopo simply lay back obligingly, crooning sweetly and making shapes with his little starfish hands while I battled resolutely on.

I had a much better success with breakfast.

'Most important meal of the day, Jopo,' I informed him, as I popped the eggs in to boil.

To tell the truth, I was playing for time. I intended settling Jopo down in front of *CBeebies* while I made another phone call to his mother. She had to be back soon, surely, or I was going to get it in the neck at work. Because unless Sharon turned up within the next half hour I was going to have to take Jopo with me.

Meanwhile, one eye fastened on Jopo, blissfully sucking up runny egg yolk from his toast soldier, I kept the other eye on the front door in the — admittedly faint — hope that Sharon would come crashing through it any minute. But in the time it took me to wash and dress myself and dislodge the dried egg yolk that appeared to have fastened itself to Jopo's hair and face, Sharon neither answered her mobile nor let herself in.

'Right then! How would you like to come and see where Cate works, Jopo?'

Jopo waggled his puppy-dog head enthusiastically.

'Shoes on then!' I trilled. 'Up sticks!'

Something was happening to my personality. I seemed to have been taken over by Super Nanny and I was scaring myself with my newly acquired chirpiness.

Ten minutes later, pushing Jopo down the road in his buggy, nappy bag swinging from side to side as we went, I masterminded my revenge on Sharon. She'd lied to me from the start, I decided, with her 'just a drink with the girls' baloney. You don't get dressed up like that for a drink with the girls unless the girls happen to be wives and girlfriends of the England football squad.

She'd gone off clubbing, all right. And she'd pulled. As had been her intention from the first She'd be back later on today looking like the cat that had got the cream, while I would be swapping Jopo for my P45. But, before that eventuality, I had some explaining to do. I was grateful that I had to manoeuvre my way through the heavy café door backwards because that way I didn't have to face Finola right away.

Let me explain: Finola Corrigan doesn't like me. Any excuse she can find to malign me to her father, who owns this place, she will seize on like a starving dog who's been let near a bone. Fortunately, Mr Corrigan likes me. Did I say, by the way, that Finola's opinion of me is reciprocated? With knobs on.

'Who's this?' she yelled.

'I know! I know! I can explain,' I said. 'And I'm sorry if I'm a bit late.'

I thought it best to appear humble at first. My plan was to let Jopo's charm do all the work. In half an hour she'd be finding him a pencil and a bit of paper to draw on and topping up his beaker with milk. But as soon as I saw the look of repulsion on her face as her eyes swept over my little trundling bundle of joy, I knew my plan had already come to grief. There are some people who don't see the point of babies. They'll drool over pictures of fluffy kittens, but present them with a child who has been abandoned by his mother and all you get is an expression of stony-faced distaste.

Fortunately, Mr C appeared just as Jopo, who — with some justification in my opinion, considering the way Finola was glaring at him — began to set up a wail.

'And who's this then? Hello, little fella! Are you looking for a job? Or is it one of these fine Chelsea buns you're after?'

Jopo's tears dried as if by magic at the

appearance of the sticky bun and, clutching it with both hands, he flopped back down in his seat. I wasn't sure it was such a good idea so soon after breakfast, but I was a girl in a fix, and if a sticky bun kept Jopo quiet for long enough for me to explain my situation, then a sticky bun it was.

Mr C was very understanding, as I'd predicted he would be.

'It won't be so bad,' he said. 'We'll manage between us. And it's just for the morning, right, Cate?'

'Right,' I said, crossing my fingers behind my back.

Finola wasn't giving in without a fight. 'Just make sure he doesn't upset the customers, that's all,' she said, sniffing, 'and don't make him an excuse not to do any work.'

Sometimes I wonder how Mr Corrigan, with his big sad eyes and his kind face, could have spawned such a mean-spirited minx as Finola.

Between us we managed fine with the breakfast rush. Jopo charmed the customers — as I'd known all along he would

— and revelled in the company. It was a joy to watch Finola's mean mouth grow thinner and thinner the more people stopped by his buggy to ruffle his curls and exchange a few words with him — well, they did the words and he offered a few grunts and giggles in return.

'He's good for business,' one little old lady said, staying longer than she'd intended and ordering another round of tea and toasted teacakes for her friend and herself. 'You should bring him in more often!'

'Hear that, Finola?' I sang out. She scrunched her face up in what I interpreted as a smile for the old lady and a glower for me — no mean feat, actually, and one that only Finola Corrigan could pull off, but said nothing. I think she knew she was on to a loser.

The tide began to turn in her favour in the run-up to the dinnertime rush, however. In order for the wheels of the Corrigan enterprise to turn smoothly, things have to run like clockwork. Preparing the lunches requires co-ordination, speed and intense concentration. There's a mountain of chopping, slicing, stirring and spreading to conquer even before the first customer arrives with his order. Between the hours of eleven and twelve you just cannot take your eye off the ball for an instant or the kitchen will descend into such turmoil that it would render Gordon Ramsay speechless.

Jopo, worn out from entertaining the customers, had fallen into a deep sleep for a good hour, and, in the lull that always happens mid-morning, things were progressing just as they usually did. Mr Corrigan popped outside for a sneaky fag and a leaf through his newspaper, Finola nipped into the back to get on with the ordering and I got on the phone to Sharon.

Once more all I got was Sharon's voicemail message.

'I'm sorry, I'm not able to get to the phone right now . . . '

'Aargh!'

I couldn't help the shriek of frustration that escaped me. What was she playing at? This was the last time I'd do any favours for Sharon, Jopo or no Jopo. She must have seen me coming, I decided. Spotted that three-letter word 'mug' stamped across my forehead the very first day she clapped eyes on me.

The café was empty apart from someone who'd been sitting hunched over an empty cup for the last twenty minutes or so. I'd noticed him come in. Tall, nice hair. Late twenties, early thirties. Casually but stylishly dressed. He'd carried *The Guardian* under his arm, which, was pretty unusual around here. When he'd first come in, Finola and I had clocked him at the same time. She'd practically sprinted across the room to reach him before I could get there first, to take his order. Most undignified, really, because he barely registered her.

He'd seen me, though. Oh, yes. His eyes had been on me all the time as I'd been going round wiping the tables. If it had been one of the blokes from the building site I'd have flicked the cloth round as quick as I could before taking refuge behind the counter, sharpish. But I made the most of this man's appreciative, yet subtle glances. It was not every day you got talent in.

He'd gone back to his paper once I'd got my phone out, but now, as I let rip with my shriek of frustration, I heard him speak.

'Sounds like you're having a few problems.'

Scraping back his chair, he got up, picking up his empty cup and saucer and bringing them over towards me. His route took him past Jopo's buggy and he had a great, slouchy, kind of walk. He — Jopo, I mean — was still asleep, but starting to make sharp little stretchy movements, and every now and then his rosebud mouth would pucker in anger and his eyelids would flicker furiously. I didn't like the look of it.

'I'm trying to get hold of his mum,' I said.

I didn't want him thinking I was a single mother, or my chances would be stymied right from the off. There must be loads of cafés he could go to for his mid-morning tea break, full of beautiful waitresses, no strings attached. The trick was to make him come back to mine.

He glanced down at Jopo, who stirred

some more, punching and jabbing at the air as he swam up from sleep.

'Not yours, then?'

'Good God, no!' I gushed.

I might have been mistaken, but I thought he looked a bit relieved. And pleased.

'Nice cup of tea, that,' he said, holding out the cup and saucer.

'Does that mean you'll be back for another, some day?'

Love him, but I think I might have embarrassed him.

'I might,' he said. 'Yeah. Definitely.'

'Good!' I said, and took the saucer.

When our hands touched it was like a current passing through us. We both snatched our fingers away, like we'd been burned. It was at that point that Jopo, having decided in his sleep that it was time for a radical change of image, let out a wail.

'I'll leave you to it, then,' he said with a nervous look at Jopo. 'Looks like you're gonna have your hands full.'

Well, that was an understatement. Jopo was frantic. Beside himself. Alternately he flailed the air with angry fists and tugged at his seat-belt, desperate to get out. I couldn't blame him. He'd been sitting down too long. When I released him I thought he might shut up, but no such luck.

'That child needs changing,' said Finola, who was back in action setting fresh cruets out. 'He stinks.'

'Volunteering, are you?' I muttered through gritted teeth.

'She's not coming back, is she? You're stuck with that kid forever, that's what I think.'

My retort was drowned out by the noise of Jopo's wails. People were starting to come in for their dinners. In half an hour this place would be as busy as the M1. 'Sharon, you are so dead,' I muttered as, carrying Jopo at arms' length, I headed for the back, nappy bag in tow.

Technically, the little back room, where we put our feet up for ten minutes when it was our turn on the rota for a break, was part of the café premises. Mr Corrigan was in there now, drawing breath before the onslaught of the ravenous hordes. If a food inspector were to walk in off the street and catch me changing Jopo's nappy, we'd be closed down like a shot.

Maybe I was being paranoid, but I'd already started to wonder about the hunky *Guardian* reader. There was something not Robinwood Estate about him. What if he was a food inspector? If he returned to pick up the newspaper he'd left on his table, and if he saw what I was doing in here, then it was all over for Mr Corrigan.

When he looked up, Mr Corrigan's eyes expressed all my own misgivings. The sight of his lugubrious face filled me with guilt at foisting Jopo on to him. But what choice did I have? I decided to appeal to his better nature.

'Honestly, Mr Corrigan. If I'd had any other choice — '

'Cate, you're going to have to find someone else to have him, you know that, don't you?'

'But I don't know anyone. Sharon's never made any mention of her mother. I wouldn't have a clue how to get hold of her.'

'What about your own mother, Cate? Couldn't she take over for a bit?'

My mother? Was he mad? Her parenting skills were worse than Sharon's. Not only that, the last time she'd been in these parts she'd broken Mr Corrigan's heart.

An irate Finola, who must have been ear-wigging all this from outside, suddenly stuck her head round the door.

'Oh, yes, Dad,' she said, her voice spitting venom. 'You'd like that, wouldn't you? That woman back in our lives again, wreaking havoc.'

Well, at least Finola and I agreed on something!

'Listen,' I said. 'It needn't come to that. Look, Jopo's happier already. We'll just sit him up at a table where I can keep an eye on him, give him his crayons and some paper and he'll be fine till the rush is over. Then I'll try Sharon's number again.'

Finola turned on her heels and stamped out and Mr C blinked at me like a man who wanted to believe but just couldn't find it in him.

'Just today, Cate,' he said. 'That's all I'm saying.'

I watched him make his way back into the kitchen and breathed an exhausted sigh.

'You've got to help me here, Jopo,' I said. 'Or we're both out.'

Jopo looked up at me for all the world as if he'd understood the gravity of the situation. Back in the café, I settled him down with a drink and his drawing stuff and got on with my job, every now and then looking up hopefully as I bustled between tables.

I began to relax. Obviously, my little sermon had done the trick. Jopo had decided to be a good boy for the rest of the afternoon. When I next rang Sharon's number she would answer in person and she'd be round here to pick him up within minutes. A tender reunion scene between mother and child would ensue, and everything would be back to normal. Except, of course, that she wouldn't be getting off that lightly from me.

I was busy putting together an order for two specials, and deciding exactly what I was going to say to Jopo's mother when she did turn up, when Finola suddenly loomed out of nowhere and grabbed me by the shoulder.

'Where is he?' she yelled. 'The boy. He's disappeared!'

2

This isn't happening, this isn't happening, this isn't happening. Like a mantra, the words played over and over in my head. Stepping over the spilled curry and rice at my feet — today's special — I darted out from behind the counter, tearing off my apron and pushing aside alarmed customers as I went. At the door I paused and tried to calm down, but my knees were knocking together alarmingly. There was no sign of Jopo whichever way I looked, but I was going to have to make a decision. Left or right? Which was it to be?

Larkin Boulevard, on which Corrigan's Café was situated, was a wide road, heaving with traffic and bustling with people at this hour. To the left was the street market and to the right were shops. Some blind impulse propelled me right. Striding down the street, I hugged myself against the cold, desperately calling Jopo's name as I went, only vaguely aware of the strange looks I was getting from passers-by.

How far could an eighteen-month-old get in two minutes? I fought off fear as long as I could, but it was hopeless. Dreadful things happened to children in the blink of an eye. I even had a horrible vision of the hooded visitor of the night before. Did he have anything to do with this?

Quickening my steps to match my breath, I battled on, my eyes roaming the road ahead. I didn't know where I was going but I knew I had to keep moving. It was the only way to quell the mounting terror threatening to overwhelm me and to trick myself into believing that Jopo had gone off of his own accord and would be round the next corner.

The whisper of a memory stopped me in my tracks. Something Sharon had told me the night before, just before she'd left. The market. I should have gone to the market first. This would be Jopo's first real Christmas, Sharon had said. Yesterday — was it really only yesterday?

— she'd taken him to the Christmas stall, where you could buy decorations. When Jopo had seen the display of fairy lights and tinsel, he'd clapped his hands in glee, she'd said, and she'd had to drag him away with promises that he could go back tomorrow.

Pivoting round, I shot off in the opposite direction. As I retraced my steps I prayed that some nice, homely stall-holder was even now firmly in control of the situation, and that it would only be a matter of moments before someone recognised him as the little boy from Corrigan's.

There was something going on in the doorway of the cafe. A huddle of people, voices raised, all cutting across each other. I picked out Finola above everyone else, then Mr Corrigan's deep, rich, smoker's chuckle, and finally another voice — well-modulated, measured — and in the middle of all of it, the sweetest sound on earth: Jopo's sing-song chatter.

I was in amongst them in a trice, snatching Jopo from the arms of the stranger without even acknowledging him. Right now I could only think of Jopo. Relief came flooding in as I hugged him close, my heartbeat so loud it pounded in my ears.

I turned on Jopo's captor. 'You'd better not have harmed him,' I yelled, smothering Jopo's head with my kisses.

'Whoa! Hold your horses! What do you think I am? I rescued him just as he was about to throw himself under a bus! If there's any harm done here you need to look at yourself first.'

There was something familiar about the face. Only, the last time I'd seen it it had been smiling and relaxed. It was my customer from earlier, the *Guardian*-carrying dish who'd set my pulse racing when he'd handed me his cup and saucer. What a difference an hour makes, I thought. And who was he calling neglectful?

'I beg your pardon! Are you saying I don't know how to look after a child?' I snapped.

'My opinion's not important,' he said. 'But you might want to consider how Social Services would look at things.'

All my puffed-up fury suddenly collapsed around me. I felt vulnerable, threatened and very, very scared.

'So you're not a food inspector, then? Is that what you're telling me? That you're from the Social Services?'

I didn't know which was worse. I'd known all along there was something funny about him, for all his banter and easy manner. It was more than I could bear when his puzzled expression switched to one of merriment.

'What? Food Inspector? Social Services? What are you on about?' he said. 'Look, I just saw him on the street. I remembered him from before. Nobody else seemed interested. When you see someone in danger, whoever it is — well, you've got to wade in, haven't you?'

My insides gave a little dip as I heard this. My very own Superman.

'Tell me you're not wearing your underpants over your trousers,' I said.

He flashed open his jacket. 'Check if you want,' he said.

No Superman tights, just a pair of figure-hugging jeans. Feeling slightly over-heated, I decided to transfer my gaze to his face. I was further enchanted by the slow, sexy grin that reached his eyes and made the skin around them crinkle ever so slightly in a way that suggested he wasn't quite as wholesome as his philosophy might suggest.

'Look,' I said, 'why don't you come back inside and I'll make you lunch on the house? Or rather, Mr Corrigan will. You wouldn't want to eat my cooking.'

It was best to get that out in the open from the off. Just because I worked in a café didn't mean I knew how to cook, so if he was looking for a domestic goddess he'd be better off looking elsewhere.

'I'd love to,' he said, as if he meant it. 'But — '

'I know,' I said, 'you've a wife and child at home waiting.'

I said I had a big mouth, didn't I? But today I was excelling myself. Losing Jopo and finding the man of my dreams all in the space of one short morning had made me delirious.

'No wife. No child. Just work,' he said. 'All this has made me late. I'm going to have to get a move on.'

He was looking at me like he didn't want to go at all. I stepped back and started to fuss over Jopo who didn't really need any fussing over, being comfortable enough hanging round my neck, his face nuzzling my cheek. But I had to do something. Otherwise, I might have found myself yelling, 'Take me with you, I'll follow you to the ends of the earth.'

The words I spoke were far more mundane, however. I thanked him for what he'd done and apologised if I'd acted a bit lairy. He accepted my thanks with a gracious shrug and brushed my apology aside with equal aplomb.

'Kid's lucky to have you watching out for him,' he said.

I grinned. 'A minute ago you said I was neglectful,' I reminded him.

'I was simply defending myself,' he said.

He seemed to be struggling a bit now. Like he had something to say but he didn't know how I'd take it. Was he about to ask me for a date? I wondered.

But then he said, 'The mother. Where exactly is she?'

The urge to blurt out that I didn't know but I wished she'd flamin' well hurry back was strong. But something stopped me. I get fed up with all the world's woes being blamed on single mums.

'You're a very loyal friend,' he said, when it became clear I thought Sharon's whereabouts were none of his business. Then he said, 'I'm going now and I don't even know your name.'

If this was a ploy to touch my hand again, I was all for it.

'Cate. Cate Minton,' I said, extending my frozen fingers.

'Tom Wilson,' he said, his hand closing over mine.

How is it, even in the middle of December, men's hands are always warm?

'Pleased to meet you, Tom Wilson,' I simpered.

From somewhere inside the café, the dulcet tones of my co-worker suddenly assaulted my ears.

'If you're not too busy out there, I'd appreciate a hand clearing these tables!'

Tom and I exchanged a secret look.

'See you around then, Cate,' he said. Chucking Jopo under the chin, he added, 'See ya, Jopo.'

I watched him stride off down the street. I'd have liked to stay and watch it till he'd rounded the corner, but duty, in the shape of Finola Corrigan, was making that impossible.

★ ★ ★

The rest of the afternoon was just hopeless. Finola lost no opportunity to have a go at me. There'd been more complaints this morning than there'd been in the whole of last year, apparently, and all of them, according to her, down to me. Dirty cutlery, dirty tables, forgotten orders or just plain wrong ones. I'm sure there was more but I've always been good at switching off. I knew what was happening. I knew what she was doing. She was punishing me for catching Tom Wilson's eye because she fancied him herself.

'Listen, Cate.'

Mr Corrigan came into the back where I was changing Jopo, between intermittent bouts of checking my phone for messages. I didn't mind upsetting Finola but I felt really bad at how much I'd mucked Mr C around this morning.

'I think you should get off early today,' he said. 'You can't keep the little 'un cooped up here all afternoon. It's not fair on him.'

'Things'll be back to normal tomorrow, Mr C,' I said, as I strapped Jopo back into his buggy. 'And I'll make it up, honest.'

I told myself I should go home, but all Jopo's paraphernalia was at Sharon's house. It was shrouded in darkness when I reached it. And Sharon still hadn't come home. Mechanically, I removed Jopo from the buggy, divested both of us of our outer garments and then went round switching on the lights, making jolly conversation like there was nothing up. But inside I was panicking.

I was definitely going to have to do something now. Things had gone far enough. Don't go to the police, the hoody from last night had said. But who was he

119

to tell me what to do? It was five o'clock. I'd give it three hours and then — if she didn't ring or turn up before then — I'd make the call. Comforted by the decision I'd made, I set about making Jopo something to eat.

Sharon's fridge yielded very little, but there was a yogurt that wasn't past its sell-by date and a bit more than a scraping of low cholesterol spread. A further search revealed a couple of tins of own-brand baked beans, half a white sliced loaf, a brown speckled banana and a couple of tangerines.

It was while I was opening and shutting cupboard doors, looking for anything of nutritional value I could feed Jopo, that I came across two huge bin bags — one filled with gift-wrapped parcels of all shapes and sizes, the other stuffed full of boxes of crackers, biscuits and chocolates and sundry tins of festive food. That's when the penny dropped. This is what Sharon had been borrowing money for. Getting herself up to her ears in debt with a loan shark just so as she could splash out on Christmas. There must have been two hundred quid's worth of food and booze here, let alone what she'd spent on presents.

'Oh, Sharon,' I muttered under my breath. 'You fool.'

The sound of breaking glass and the landing of a heavy object, closely followed by the sound of crockery cascading to the floor, sent me running into the kitchen, my heart in my mouth for the second time that day.

My first thought was that Jopo had climbed on to a chair to reach for something, had fallen and was now lying comatose on the hard kitchen floor. Just how were people expected to cope with being parents? I asked myself.

But it wasn't Jopo on the floor, and for that I was hugely relieved. My relief lasted precisely thirty seconds — the time it took my eyes to take in the mayhem and ascertain its true cause. The kitchen window had been smashed, and shards of glass, mixed up with bits of broken crockery, lay scattered all over the floor. Cautiously, I approached the missile that had wreaked this havoc. It was an ordinary house brick, a scrap of paper around it, held on by an innocuous looking black rubber band.

This is your first warning, it read. *You've got 24 hours to pay up or else.*

It was then that I had a truly shocking thought. What if Sharon, knowing there was a time limit on this debt, hadn't gone out clubbing at all? What if, instead of spending money, she'd been making money?

Sharon had left full-time education before her sixteenth birthday. She'd never done a job of work in her life. But there was one job where the only qualification you needed was to be female. It was an added bonus if you were young and pretty. I prayed to God, if he was listening, that she hadn't gone down that road, but if she was desperate, who knew what lengths she'd go to?

★ ★ ★

'Did the police say when they'd be round?'

Mr Corrigan sat at the kitchen table

dunking a ginger biscuit in the steaming cup of tea I'd made him, after taking no time at all to fix Sharon's broken window. I don't know what impulse had driven me to ring him for help, but I was glad I had. That enviable quality he possessed of calmness in the face of adversity was now rubbing off on me. My knees had practically stopped knocking, along with my heart against my ribs.

'Oh, you know what they're like.' I was hedging furiously. 'They'll probably get round to paying me a visit about this time tomorrow.'

Only they wouldn't be because I hadn't rung them. What was holding me back? I was a law-abiding citizen. I paid my taxes and I never crossed the road without getting the nod from the little green man.

Before the brick had landed I'd promised myself that by eight o'clock, if Sharon still hadn't turned up, I'd report her missing. I'd done her enough favours, I'd decided. But since my latest suspicion about Sharon had reared its ugly head, the prospect of involving the law was becoming even less attractive. There'd be some do-gooder from Social Services demanding poor little innocent Jopo as a sacrifice. And what good would that do him?

I couldn't let them take Jopo away. He had his own things in his own little world. Sharon wasn't a bad mother. Most of the stuff I'd discovered she'd bought to make Jopo's Christmas special. There was hardly anything for herself, apart from the odd box of chocolates, and a bottle of wine. But Social Services would take a dim view of prostitution and who could blame them?

Maybe if I hadn't experienced being in care myself at first hand — albeit very briefly — I might have felt differently about making that call. After all, they weren't monsters but good people — there to help as best they could when kids found themselves let down by those who were supposed to put them first. But no kid, looking back on the events that had removed them from their home, was ever going to regard the authorities as having their best interests at heart. I spoke as one who knew.

'What about tomorrow, Cate? What plans have you made for Jopo?'

Mr Corrigan's words broke into the hazy memory I was doing my best yet failing to stave off . . . A shadowy female figure in a shapeless coat, smelling of mints. Helping herself to my toys, as if she knew better than me what I could least bear to be parted from. Someone — was it my mother or was it this stranger? — re-assuring me it was for the best. Then the long drive through the night in the overheated car, the strange building with its unfamiliar smells and slamming doors that penetrated my troubled sleep in a strange bed, surrounded by children I didn't know . . .

'You know, I wasn't joking when I suggested you phoned your mum,' Mr C went on.

'Me and my mum,' I bantered. 'We haven't got that sort of a relationship.'

'That doesn't mean to say she wouldn't help you if she could, I bet.'

He was right. My mother had been hovering on the threshold of my life for as long as I could remember, knowing damn well there was no invite because of what she'd done, but forever hopeful that one day I might just leave the door enough ajar for her to get a foot inside. I wasn't proud of myself for the way I played her. But when you've had as little power as I'd had in my life, it felt good to be the one in charge at last.

'I'm not sure where she's living right now,' I mumbled. 'She moves around a lot.'

Mr C was looking right through me. I could tell it was puzzling him, the way I referred to my own flesh and blood like they were some casual acquaintance I really didn't feel the need to account for.

'You told me she was right here in Bursden only about six weeks ago,' he said. 'Working at the Flying Horse. She bought you a drink. You had a chat.'

She'd chatted, I'd sat stony-faced and wondered when she was going to start showing her age.

'Did I?'

On this dire performance, practising my Oscar acceptance speech was going to be a complete waste of time. Fortunately, a sudden knocking on the front door took the spotlight off me, which was a bit of a relief for about a quarter of a second till it occurred to me it might be Sharon's loan shark again. Then I went to pieces.

'I'll go.' Mr Corrigan got up from the table. He didn't seem remotely worried. 'You go up and get Jopo's stuff.'

The sooner I was in my own home the better, I decided as, shaky once more, I took the stairs two at a time. As I packed Jopo's bits and pieces, I blessed Mr Corrigan for dropping everything and running over here to help me the way he had. Finola was lucky to have a father like Mr C, if only she knew it. Nothing ever fazed him, nothing was ever too much trouble, and whatever you did wrong you'd know he'd still be there for you.

My own dad was just a distant memory now, but he'd had none of those qualities. Mostly he'd ignored me and left my upbringing to Gran, his mother. Perhaps I reminded him too much of his flighty wife. Between the two of us we'd cramped her style, which is why we'd both been left behind when she'd decided to run off.

Then Dad had got ill and died which left just Gran and me. Gran was dead too these past five years. I still lived in the council house she'd moved into after the war. She brought me up and I should have been grateful she'd got me out of care as soon as she found out about it. But a child soon understands when duty and not love motivates the one who cares for them and I was no exception. When she'd died I didn't grieve as much as perhaps I should, although it wasn't for want of trying to understand her point of view.

On my way out of Jopo's room, the sound of mingled laughter climbed the stairs to meet me. I stiffened, straining my ears to hear more of that oh-so-familiar, female, cracked plate of a laugh. Oh no! It was my mother, or I was the fairy on top of the Christmas tree.

3

'Did you ring her? After everything I said?' Perhaps it was unfair to vent my fury on Mr C. But where my mother was concerned fairness didn't come into it. Not when it was her fault I'd been put into care all those years ago. He stood there shuffling his feet and looking shame-faced. 'I thought it for the best, Cate,' he said, addressing the floor. 'If I'd had any other choice . . . '

It hadn't escaped my notice that my mother had arrived accompanied by a small suitcase.

'I wouldn't have thought looking after children was up your street, Ange,' I snapped. For good measure, I added, 'I can't pay you, you know.'

I'll say this for my mother, she is not easily ruffled. She simply tossed her still ample, still jet-black hair, darted a smouldering look sideways at Mr C and simpered at me. A glance at Mr C revealed he'd fallen under her spell already. And there was I mistaking him for a man of discernment and intelligence.

'I'll leave you two girls to sort yourselves out,' he mumbled, making a quick exit.

'I know you don't want me here, Cate.' There was a weary note in my mother's voice. 'But your boss was very persuasive. And I can see for myself you're in dire straits.'

'Oh, really? Weren't they some Eighties pop group?'

I know, I know. It was a childish remark that was beneath me. How come, whenever I got within three feet of my mother, I became thirteen again?

Her smile was an understanding one. It said, 'You've been under a lot of strain so I'll pretend I haven't heard your little outburst.' It made her look good and me pathetic.

'You can stay for one night,' I said. 'Only so as I don't have to let Mr Corrigan down, of course.'

'Of course,' she said, failing pathetically

to keep the delight out of her voice.

Jopo, tired of watching cartoons, waddled into the kitchen, trailing his stuffed dog behind him. Now we had no choice but to be civil to each other. If Supernanny had popped by at that moment she'd have been proud of the way we both united in chivvying Jopo over all the hurdles of his evening routine. It was only later, when we'd successfully negotiated the move from Sharon's house to mine, and put Jopo to bed, that the already dodgy seams of our relationship began to unravel in a few more places.

'So what's the story with his mum, then?'

She was standing by the cooker watching a pan of milk come to the boil. She'd spooned instant coffee into two mugs.

Remarkably at first, I restrained myself from asking her if the story was a familiar one. But from the excessive way she threw herself into clearing up after she'd poured the milk, it was clear the similarity wasn't lost on her.

'Did she give you any hint that she

wouldn't be coming back last night?'

'Perhaps she didn't think she needed to give a reason,' I said. 'You didn't.'

She blew the froth from her cup and a speck landed on her nose. The sight of her standing there, exposed like that, both irritated and moved me.

'Can we not leave our differences to one side, Cate?' she said with a loud sigh. 'I did wrong but, for goodness' sake, it was a lifetime ago. We all make mistakes.'

'Mothers aren't allowed to make mistakes,' I snapped. I turned and grabbed hold of the nearest tea-towel and threw it at her. 'You've got froth on your nose.'

Almost imperceptibly she turned her mouth up at the corners. Setting down her drink on the table, she wiped the froth away.

'Better now?'

I nodded, my mouth a grim line.

'God help you if you ever have kids, Cate,' she said with a weary smile. 'You'll put yourself into an early grave if you believe that.'

'It's what Gran believed,' I snapped.

'She put me first, second and third.'

She wasn't smiling any more. I'd finally goaded her. And I was glad.

'That woman only ever put herself first in all the years I knew her. She enjoyed nothing more than coming between me and your father. He was a different man when we first met,' she said.

I ducked at the change in her voice. When Gran was alive, the mere mention of Mum's name always seemed to turn her face sour and I soon learned not to speak of her.

Mum could look just as sour and had always been less than fulsome in her praise of her mother-in-law, but she'd never actually spoken ill of her till now.

'We had a ball, the pair of us. He was full of life. Full of spirit. And then we moved back here to Bursden to be with his mother.' She twisted the tea-towel in her hands as she spoke.

'She controlled him,' she went on. 'Sucked the life out of him. She wanted to do the same to me, only I wouldn't let her.'

I kept my eyes fastened on Mum's

hands as she twisted the tea-towel till her knuckles were white. I didn't want to believe any of this and yet at the same time it all made perfect sense. Then, taking myself in hand, I reminded myself that Mum was the villain of the piece.

'You put me into care,' I hissed. 'Gran went round there in person and demanded they returned me,' I said.

It was a familiar story I'd been told so many times, I might have been there.

'I was barely twenty, Cate. I was a girl, with all my future spread out before me. I wanted the two of us to take a chance on life, but your gran was a canny one. She knew that would mean leaving her out of things. So she set herself up against me. And won.'

'You've never said any of this before,' I said angrily. 'You're making it all up.'

'I'm only saying it now, reluctantly,' she said. 'I know how much your gran did for you. She was an old lady and it couldn't have been easy for her.'

What she said next stunned me. 'I pleaded with your dad. I wanted us to move right away, all three of us. Make a new start. But he wouldn't leave his mother. I couldn't take you with me, Cate. I had no money. No job. Nothing. He said — we agreed — that your security was paramount. He'd look after you, he said. But in the end he couldn't manage it.'

She let go of the tea-towel and it floated to the ground. And then she delivered the final, knockout blow.

'It was your dad who put you into care, Cate. Not me.'

★   ★   ★

Next day at work I taxied along on autopilot, skilfully deflecting enquiries from Mr C about whether or not the police had paid me a visit. Thanks to the demand for mince pies and turkey baguettes, standing still and doing nothing was not an option, so even last night's conversation with my mother remained firmly tucked away at the back of my mind.

It was harder to ignore Finola, however. It took her no time to worm it out of me that Sharon still wasn't back. Then my mother popped in with Jopo.

'Take five minutes if you want, Cate,' Finola said with unheard-of graciousness.

'Is that the daughter?' Mum asked me, when I took her a cup of tea and Jopo a biscuit.

I slid down into a chair, grateful to take the weight off my feet, and took Jopo on to my lap.

'Is it me you've come to see or Mr Corrigan?' I said, taking in the painted nails and the sexy ankle boots.

'Don't be silly, Cate,' she said, blowing madly on her tea. 'We're on the way to the park and we thought we'd stop by, that's all.'

'In those heels?' I smirked.

She didn't fool me, and when Mr C — who'd been out at the suppliers' for the past couple of hours — pushed open the door of the café, it was clear my suspicions had been correct. She suddenly sat up straight, crossed her legs and thrust out her chest. Mr C responded by ducking his head, rolling his eyes and breaking into a grin that seemed to slide all over his face. The mating ritual of the elder, wrinkly singleton. My mum did flirting like most other people did breathing. And the effect on Mr C was dramatic. In the space of five minutes he shed twenty years, I swear.

Since they were obviously getting on like a chip-pan on fire, I decided I might as well leave them to it. Perhaps I was jealous that my mother had got herself an admirer, because I found myself suddenly thinking of Tom Wilson. He'd been keen enough yesterday, so why hadn't he returned as he'd practically promised?

After Mum and Jopo left, the atmosphere in the café returned more or less to normal, though Mr C was still more pumped up than usual and Finola was still being suspiciously nice to me. I just put my head down and got on with it, putting their change of mood down to Christmas, which was just around the corner now.

But by the time we pulled down the blinds at the end of the day, there'd been no sign of Tom, and it was somewhat forlornly that I dragged my weary body down the street and home. Funny, all day I hadn't given a thought to Sharon. She'd been away two full days and one night and I hadn't heard a peep from her. How long would it be before Mum decided to go over my head and get in touch with the police herself? I wondered.

* * *

I panicked when I saw the car parked outside my front door. It looked worryingly official. I let myself into the house, making as little noise as I could. The houses on Robinwood all open straight on to the living room, but the voices I heard came from the kitchen. Tiptoeing across the floor, I put my ear to the kitchen door. Two women — my mother and someone I didn't know.

I had less than a moment to pull away from the door before it opened to reveal a woman in her fifties. She had social worker stamped all over her. 'Oh, here's my daughter back from work!' said Mum lightly. I opened my mouth to speak, but from behind the woman's back Mum put her finger to her lips and shook her head. 'I'll just show our visitor out and then I'll get the tea on,' she said, almost pushing the woman towards the door.

I was still standing stock-still with my coat and scarf on, keys in hand, when the traitor returned.

'What have you done?' My voice trembled as I tried to control my anger for Jopo's sake.

'Thank God she's gone,' was Mum's reply, but she didn't fool me.

'You promised you wouldn't butt in!' I was practically shaking with fury now.

Mum was very soon as livid as me, accusing me of jumping to conclusions. This social worker had had nothing to do with her, she insisted. She'd just turned up out of the blue when she'd been in the middle of watching *Loose Women*.

'Well, she wouldn't just turn up here uninvited, would she?' I snapped.

'Don't point the finger in my direction! I gave her short shrift, let me tell you. Told her Sharon had gone away to visit friends for a few days and had made proper arrangements with you and me.

Believe me, Cate, it's the truth.'

All the little cogs in my brain suddenly started going round at once.

'Finola!'

Well, it certainly explained the grotesque charm offensive she'd been working on me all day.

I looked at her and thought that, actually, she was someone to be proud of.

'I'm sorry I blamed you, Mum. You've been a brick.'

She tried to look as though what I'd said wasn't a big deal, but I could see it was from the way her neck went bright crimson.

'Hot flush?' I asked her, giving her a way out, adding, 'I've let it go on too long, haven't I?'

'You were never to blame for anything that went wrong in our family, Cate,' she replied.

And then we were hugging and laughing and crying. And then there was smoke rising from one of the frying-pans and goodness knows what disaster might have followed if Jopo hadn't toddled in just then and started jumping up and down and clapping his hands. In the end, we had beans on toast. And by the time I'd chased the last bean round the plate and mopped up the last bit of brown sauce with my final corner of toast, I'd come to a decision.

'I'm going to go round to Sharon's right away and I'm going to phone the police, as well,' I said. 'That's something else I've left too long. I should have phoned them sooner.'

'You were protecting Jopo, Cate,' Mum said. 'Nobody would blame you.'

She really was on my side, I decided, as with grim determination I set my shoulders against the bracing air and crossed the road, pulling my coat around me and digging inside my pocket for Sharon's spare key.

It was then I realised that no key was needed. Sharon's door was already ajar. Jammed halfway through the letter-box, a piece of paper was sticking out at right angles. I guessed immediately it was another threat. With trepidation I put out my shaking hand and removed the note and opened it.

This is your second warning, it said.

I was so deep in thought, wondering what on earth I was expected to do next, that at first I didn't register the sound of the car engine as it roared up alongside me. But as the wheels screeched to a halt and the door slammed I became frozen to the spot, as footsteps came towards me.

'Cate! Are you all right? What's happened?' It was Tom Wilson.

'I wasn't going to go in alone,' I said with a grim smile.

'Well, you won't need to now,' he said, applying his boot to the door with a swift kick. Did he know something I didn't?

'You don't think there's anyone still there, do you?'

I was hanging on to his sleeve, but so far he hadn't shaken me off, so until he did I was staying put.

'Light's on the left. Just there,' I prompted.

He soon located it and switched it on and we both drew stunned breaths. The place had been ransacked. Whoever had been in here had decided to teach Sharon a lesson all right. There was even a spray-painted message on the wall. *Happy Christmas! Thanks 4 the prezzies!* it said.

'The pig has taken his loan back in kind,' I fumed, explaining everything I'd suspected about the trouble Sharon had got herself into, borrowing money she couldn't afford to pay back, then doing a runner out of fear of being caught up with.

Reluctantly, I let go of Tom's sleeve and scurried straight to the kitchen cupboard, where Sharon had been painstakingly stashing her Christmas booty for who knows how many weeks, and went to open it.

'Don't touch anything, Cate,' Tom yelled, close at my heels.

Ever since he'd turned up in his car so dramatically, like the Sweeney in all those reruns, there'd been something odd about Tom's behaviour. Either he watched too many cop shows or he'd been trained to case a room. All that flattening himself against the wall with his head pointing one way and his eyes another had made me smell a rat.

'Fingerprints,' he said.

'Now why didn't I think of that?'

My manner was flippant while I endeavoured to quell my suspicions. It was a relief when my phone went.

'That'll be my mother wondering where I've got to,' I muttered.

It took a while to register who it really was shrieking at me over my phone.

'Sharon! Where are you! You've got to come home now. Right away!'

Sharon was clearly beside herself. Between apologising and asking after Jopo, she kept telling me how low her battery was.

'Where are you, Sharon?' I repeated. 'Just tell me and I'll come and get you.'

At this she became almost hysterical.

'No! I can't say where. He'll find out, Cate, and then he'll come and get me. That's why I couldn't tell you, don't you see? He'd get it out of you and then he'd come for me.'

'Get a name,' Tom hissed.

'Any minute now,' I thought, 'He's going to launch himself on me. In other circumstances that would be a good thing.' But I was sure it was just my phone he wanted and a chance to talk to Sharon. And I was beginning to see why.

'Who exactly is after you, Sharon?' I asked her.

'I can't say, Cate.'

Tom shook his head sorrowfully.

'Ask her if it's Mick Foster,' he mouthed.

I obliged.

'How'd you know that?' she said.

Like I said, Sharon wasn't very bright. Mick Foster had been well and truly grassed up. But Sharon's phone was suddenly dead.

'You're a policeman, aren't you?' I said. 'Help us out here and get your mates to trace this call.'

★   ★   ★

Hours later, I was still coming to terms with the realisation that the man I'd fancied ever since I first set eyes on him was a policeman, working undercover, and that knowing that didn't make me fancy him any less. Tom knew all about Mick Foster and his nasty, extortionate ways and had been after him for months. Now he had the evidence and Mick Foster was already in custody.

Sharon's call had been traced to a house on the other side of town, where she'd been hiding with a friend she'd been in care with. Now she was reunited with Jopo — sleeping on my sofa for a change, in a neat twist of coincidences. My mother, not wanting to inconvenience me any further, or so she said — though privately I think she had designs of her own — had kindly taken up Mr C's offer of a lift back to her place.

It was gone midnight when Tom knocked on my door. He looked tired, and a bit hangdog. But it didn't make a scrap of difference to the effect he was having on me.

'I can't let you in,' I said. 'Sharon's here and if she sees you she'll think you've come to arrest her.'

He smiled at me quizzically. 'I'm not in uniform, Cate,' he said.

'You think that makes a difference? Sharon can smell an officer of the law at fifty paces.'

He looked sad. 'So you don't want to see me again, then?'

Something magical stirred inside me, the swoop of a bird, the dive of a fish.

'I'm a detective, Cate,' he went on. 'But what I can't work out is how you feel. Does it make any difference to us, me being a copper?'

To us, he'd said. To us. I thought about it for at least — ooh, thirty seconds — letting my eyes wander all over his face. I knew my answer really mattered to him. But I had a question of my own, too.

'Does it matter that I work in a backstreet café for a minimum wage?'

He shook his head, wrinkled his brow, and gave me a 'Why would it?' kind of look.

'Well then,' I said.

'Well then, indeed,' he said, taking my hand. 'What are we waiting for?'

A Village Affair

1

Cristyne's anticipation over her date with Darren later that evening had dominated her thoughts from her first moment of waking and she'd thought of little else all day. So much so that even the chores she usually found so tedious and time-consuming failed to make a dent in her good mood.

When she was as excited as now, sprinting from the bus station to La Casa, the bar in town Darren had suggested as their meeting place, she wondered why she'd ever considered packing in her job as an au pair and returning to Berlin so soon after she'd arrived on British shores.

All that moping about in her room feeling homesick for Germany was a thing of the past now, definitely. There was plenty wrong with England — buses that never ran on time for one thing, making her already five minutes late. But when the sun shone, Quantock-cum-Steeple was as picturesque and cosy as the village in those dubbed inspector Barnaby dramas she used to watch with her mother back home. Without all the murders, obviously, thank goodness!

She had no complaints about her English family either; at least, not about Mrs Ford — Alana — who was sweet and kind and patient with Cristyne whenever she got mixed up with her English. Only this morning she'd jumped to her defence when Mr Ford — Edgar and 'my other half', as Alana jokingly called him — criticised her for some silly grammar mistake she'd made.

'You'll have to excuse Edgar, Cristyne,' she'd said, her eyes bright and her tone mischievous. 'He's a barrister, and all barristers are insufferable snobs when it comes to the English language. You'd think it had been handed down from God along with the Ten Commandments and the rules about the right way to pass the port.'

Edgar had drawn his lips back in a smile at this, but his eyes were cold. He'd left for work then, thank goodness, and the tension that was always in the air when he was about — which, thankfully, due to his profession wasn't often — dissolved.

Cristyne glanced at her watch anxiously. She hadn't even reached the High Street yet and she was getting a stitch in her side with the effort of running. This evening, before she left the house, she'd put on make-up and now she suspected the foundation and blusher she'd applied so carefully were melting with all this unaccustomed physical exertion.

She told herself to relax. Darren knew what the buses were like more than she did, probably. Of course he'd wait for her. She wished she didn't always feel so anxious when it came to men, but the truth was she'd had little experience of dating. At school she'd been too serious, hard-working and, yes, too plain, to be part of the popular gang and had never learned to flirt.

No one had been more surprised than Cristyne herself when Darren had stood her a drink at the bar the night she'd popped into The Eagle and Child, just to see the inside of a real English village pub, so she could write home and tell her mum about it. She'd expected horse brasses and a log fire with maybe a picture of the Queen on the wall and a dartboard, and had been disappointed by the pub's lack of real character. It could have been any bar in the district of Berlin where she lived, apart from the language and the shape of the glasses, and the fact that you were expected to pay for your drink immediately and not at the end of the evening as was the custom at home.

Darren had approached her just as she'd got to the bottom of her cola and was on the verge of leaving because she felt foolish standing at the bar all alone.

'Don't go yet,' he said. 'Let me buy you another drink. A proper one this time.'

Had she been back in her own country, she'd have refused without hesitation. She wasn't the type of girl who allowed herself to be picked up by strange men. But this was England and she was having an adventure, independent for the first time in her life. And if at any time she felt threatened, well, she could always leave by the front door and be back home in less than two minutes.

In the end, she stayed another two hours and the time flew by. Darren had spotted her about the village, he said, pushing a buggy with another couple of kids in tow. Was it true she was working as a nanny for that rich family, who lived in the big, secluded house with the Range Rover and the Merc clogging up the drive?

She'd enjoyed the fact that her job impressed him, though she'd had to put him right about the difference between Nanny and au pair. This was just a temporary job. She had no intentions of ending up in a career where she looked after other people's children for the rest of her life, she said.

Oddly, he hadn't been as interested in her plans to study medicine at university when she'd done her year au pairing as he was in her day-to-day life with the Fords and her description of their house and grounds.

But that was Englishmen for you, she decided. They didn't seem to like clever women. She should have worked that out as soon as she met Edgar, who treated the lounge like a courtroom, parading up and down while he voiced his opinion on everything from global warming to the National Health Service. Opinions always mildly tolerated, never challenged by Alana, who looked like she'd heard it all before a million times.

Cristyne had reached the High Street at last. She could see the wine bar up ahead on the opposite side of the street. Before she made her entrance she absolutely had to check out her appearance. She stopped in front of a lit-up shop window and peered at her reflection in the glass. Unfortunately, she'd have to do.

Her eyes strayed from her own reflection to that of a figure she was certain she recognised. Mesmerised, she watched him hold the door of a small, expensive-looking restaurant across the road while a woman emerged. He took her arm and the two of them made their way down the street, heads and hands touching, their peals of laughter suddenly drowned out by passing traffic.

It was as if the train of excitement Cristyne had been riding all day had suddenly slammed on the brakes before pitching her unstoppably into a wall of chaotic emotions.

How could Edgar do this to his wife? Why would he? It was just too much to take in. Thank God she only had a few more steps to take before she reached her destination. What she'd just seen had thoroughly shaken her. She needed to sit down and recover her composure. The only thing that kept her moving forward was the thought that once she arrived at La Casa she'd be able to share the experience with another person.

★　★　★

It was only when she'd replaced the receiver that Stevie realised she maybe should have waited till Kieran got home rather than ring him now to tell him her news. He might have been in the middle of an important meeting, or — horrors — behind the wheel.

Not that he'd ever have picked up if

that were the case. Kieran would never put himself at risk now he had Erin to think about. Their baby was far too precious to him. It was Erin that had brought them down here to Quantock-cum-Steeple in the first place. So that she could have the same kind of idyllic childhood Kieran had enjoyed in the exact same village where he'd grown up.

And Stevie had gone along with Kieran's dream. Of course she had. Because Stevie loved Kieran more than anyone in the world — Erin excepted, but that was a different kind of love. She'd followed him back to the part of the country he still regarded as home without question. Immediately she laid eyes on the village with the funny, quaint name, she knew, like Kieran, that it was the right place to bring up a child. It was just going to take a bit of getting used to, that was all.

Stevie wouldn't have dreamed of ringing Kieran during the day back when they lived in London and her job in a busy department store occupied her just as fully as Kieran's new business venture did him. But that's what relocating to Quantock-cum-Steeple had done to her. This little visit from her mum had suddenly taken on massive proportions because it was the most exciting thing that had happened to her in weeks.

Kieran hadn't been at all cross with her for ringing him, actually. Kieran wasn't the type to get cross at all. Not even when — as had happened this morning — Stevie hadn't got round to ironing a shirt for him and he couldn't put his hands on a clean pair of underpants.

It was hard for her getting up night after night to feed Erin, he said. Being a mother to a small and voraciously greedy infant was a demanding job. Good Lord, if he thought he was ever going to turn into one of those husbands who relinquished responsibility for his own day-to-day requirements, like men of his father's generation, then Stevie had every right to hit him over the head with a club. Besides, he quite liked the idea of going commando for the day. It made him feel like a gun-slinging Alpha Male, and when you were setting out into the big, bad, old world to meet your first prospective client, and you were quaking in your boots, then you needed all the macho back-up you could get.

She suspected Kieran was secretly delighted that Grace was about to pay them another visit — her second since they'd moved. Good heavens, was it already six weeks ago that they'd arrived in Quantock-cum-Steeple?

Back then they were still living out of boxes and Stevie was struggling to get Erin into any kind of routine at all. Grace had instigated a regime of regular, nutritious meals for the adults while laying the foundations for domestic order and launching a nursery routine that Mary Poppins would have been proud of.

During the fortnight she remained in charge, Erin thrived on regular bedtimes and long bouts of fresh air. She even began to enjoy bath time. The knock-on effect on Stevie's wellbeing had been remarkable. She began to feel human again — positive that they'd make a success of village life and that it was only a matter of time before she made new friends. Grace's visit had even temporarily revived their sex life.

Within hours of Grace's departure, however, all traces of the routine she'd stamped on the Masters' household vanished like a puff of smoke, and back inside crept the old enemies — fatigue, faint-heartedness, fast food and lack of libido.

'She's like Supernanny 911,' Stevie muttered on the phone to Kieran. 'She'll be back with her computer and a file full of evidence to prove what bad parents we are.'

'You're right,' Kieran replied. 'We'll both be on the naughty step.'

They snorted with giggles then, like two hysterical teenagers backing each other up in their bad behaviour. But underlying their complicity, Stevie sensed that Kieran would be just as pleased to see Grace back as she would — even if it were for different reasons. He'd get his shirts ironed and his belly filled and she'd be able to say what she really felt about Kieran's precious Quantock-cum-Steeple. Because the truth was, she still didn't know a soul in the village, even though she'd promised Grace she'd take Erin along to the mums and toddlers' meetings at the village hall. She'd tried it, she truly had, but every mother there seemed to be about eighteen, which left Stevie, at thirty-two, feeling ancient. Not ancient enough to join the Mothers' Union, however, which seemed the only other alternative for women like herself who belonged to that rare group nowadays, the stay-at-home mums.

'Why don't you invite your neighbour in for tea one day?' Grace had suggested on her last visit. 'Women of that age love cooing at babies.'

Margaret next door was probably the same age as Grace, but Grace wore suits and lipstick and Chanel perfume — even on a trip to the Post Office — and wouldn't have been seen dead in artificial fibres, so there was no way Stevie was going to risk pointing out that particular fact.

It was all right for her mother to suggest inviting people in for coffee. Grace's house was immaculate. She always had a home-baked cake to hand for the casual visitor. Plus she'd never run out of milk or sugar — or coffee and clean mugs for that matter. But to Stevie, just the thought of someone like Margaret — who probably made her own jam and churned her own butter — crossing her threshold made her nervous. So far, she'd settled for calling out a cheerful hello if she saw her neighbour in the garden on those occasions she'd dashed out to snatch the washing from the line. Washing that more often than not had already been languishing there for days and only the necessity of a clean sleep suit for Erin propelled her outside to retrieve it.

By coincidence, Margaret was in her front garden half an hour later, when Stevie, with a sinking heart, set out for the village shop. Up a ladder propped against her garage, actually, which made Stevie, who had no head for heights, feel rather queasy. Admittedly, it wasn't a very tall ladder, but all the same, she had to crane her neck when she called hello.

'Just getting rid of some of this overhang,' Margaret, dressed in her usual nondescript frock and sturdy shoes, called out, tugging heftily with a gloved hand at a clump of leaves. 'It's getting so I can hardly get in or out these days.'

Once again, Stevie noticed how perfectly friendly the village folk were if she spoke first. It was simply that she always had to speak first, or risk not being spoken to at all. Just wait till her mother visited again! She decided to put a bet on with her. If she could get Margaret to pay them a social call or to invite either Stevie or her mother inside for tea, then she'd treat Grace to the most expensive bottle of wine the village shop had to offer. Not that there'd be much choice, she thought glumly.

Stevie's heart sank deeper as the *For Sale* sign that had been hanging outside the shop ever since they'd first arrived in the village — and who knew how long before — loomed into view.

Propelling herself inside the narrow doorway backwards, dragging the buggy in after her, Stevie, her imagination working overtime, contemplated the delights she would like to find on the shelves. Fresh bagels, a dozen varieties of olive, stinky cheese and Italian cured meats. And then there were tartes tatins and fresh pesto. Heaven! But this was not the corner of London where she and Kieran had been in the habit of picking up culinary treats they could have on their plates within minutes of arriving home. If the shelves of the only grocery store in the village groaned, it certainly wasn't under the weight of a variety of produce. More likely with embarrassment at the lack of choice, Stevie mused, as she travelled along the aisles trying to choose between several packets of the most boring biscuits imaginable and two brands of breakfast cereal, both of which were cornflakes.

When she reached the bakery section, she could have cried. She'd have killed for a fresh-baked loaf, still warm and smelling slightly yeasty. But what little was on the shelf was pre-wrapped and factory-made. Maybe she should have a go at making her own bread, as Grace had shown her last time she was here. But no, that wasn't going to happen. There was only room for one domestic goddess in her family.

From the corner of her eye, Stevie spotted a packet of something that looked suspiciously like croissants. Lit up by the exact same flame of desire she remembered from her days browsing for clothes on Oxford Street, she reached out to grab it. The flame turned out to be a damp squib, however, once she discovered she wasn't the only person in competition for the goods. She suddenly found herself embroiled in an unseemly tussle with another woman, whose hand had appeared through the gap on the other side of the aisle at the same time as her own. Backwards and forwards went the croissants till Stevie, hot with embarrassment at the ridiculousness of the situation, let go at the exact same time as her rival, who'd exploded in a fizz of laughter.

'Wait there!' The other woman pushed aside a loaf. Through the space it left, a pair of merry eyes sparkled a friendly greeting. 'I'm coming round,' she added.

Alana Ford, which was how she introduced herself, refused to take no for an answer when Stevie said she really didn't mind not having the croissants. It was only fair to share, she said, insisting that Stevie came back to her house for coffee where they could guzzle them with jam before anyone else — husbands, for instance — got their mitts on them.

By the time they'd reached Alana's house, Stevie felt she'd found a friend. They seemed to have so much in common — both with babies the same age, though Alana also had two older children already in school, and both with past lives in London, working in retail.

It was nice to be able to have a good moan about the shop with someone who didn't take it as a personal criticism, as Kieran always seemed to whenever she compared Quantock-cum-Steeple unfavourably to the metropolis, and it was fun to discuss the changes they'd make if they ran it, the list of foodstuffs they'd offer becoming hilariously more and more outlandish.

Stevie assumed Alana would live in a house like hers and Kieran's — small, square and with a garden the size of a pocket-handkerchief. But as they approached a large detached building surrounded by high walls, Stevie realised that the social and financial gulf between this barrister's wife and herself was greater than anything she could have imagined from their recent encounter, when she'd been drawn to Alana's infectious giggle and bohemian appearance.

Not only that, but Alana employed an au pair, a big, sturdy German girl who seemed capable of anything, producing coffee, refusing a croissant in favour of a chocolate biscuit, then disappearing with a pile of ironing while Alana and Stevie chattered on, babies propped on their laps.

She didn't want to leave at all, but Erin was getting restless, and besides, Stevie looked forward to lots more coffee mornings with her new-found friend — who gave the impression of sharing her wishes — and she didn't want to outstay her welcome.

Phone numbers were exchanged alongside a return invitation from Stevie for a morning soon after her mum had gone back home. Her mood was buoyant and she set off homeward, with a spring in her step. But her steps slowed as, back on her own street, she neared Margaret's house. Something wasn't quite right. Why was Margaret's front door wide open, for one thing? And what on earth was that ladder doing on its side? And wasn't that one of Margaret's very own sturdy feet sticking out beneath it with the rest of her following on?

In a trice, Stevie was crouching at Margaret's side. According to her neighbour, there was no harm done. She'd taken a bit of a tumble and she'd get up in a minute, but, really, there was absolutely no need for any fuss.

Stevie was prepared to believe her, until Margaret, in an attempt to get up, swayed and staggered this way and that before finally landing in Stevie's arms. Alarmed, Stevie immediately called an ambulance and within minutes one was on its way. She felt guilty that she couldn't go with Margaret to the hospital, but by this time Erin, fed up with no longer being the centre of her mother's attention, was demanding lunch.

'I'll come and visit you just as soon as I

can,' Stevie called out as Margaret waved her a grateful goodbye.

Funny, but from having no friends at all, Stevie suddenly had two. Village life was definitely looking up, she decided, as she wheeled the buggy containing the now howling Erin round to the side gate that led to the back of the house, her preferred route in and out with the muddy buggy, so she could leave it folded up in the uncarpeted conservatory.

She could have sworn she'd closed the gate behind her on her way out. Closed it and checked she'd closed it, too. Living in London, she was paranoid where security was concerned.

'Shush, sweetheart. Home now. Safe and sound!'

She spoke to calm herself as much as Erin. Lifting her from the buggy and hugging her warm body tight, she approached the back door. It was still locked, thank goodness. But of course it was! This was Quantock-cum-Steeple, not London.

Then something crunched beneath her feet and she realised she was treading glass. Stevie let out a frightened gasp. Someone had broken into her house!

* * *

Edgar threw his keys down on to the kitchen surface. From upstairs came the sound of splashing water mingled with the sound of voices raised in fun. Alana loved bathing the boys. This was one job she never allocated to the au pair.

Cristyne was at the sink, hands immersed in water. Headphones clamped in her ears. He enjoyed watching her jump and spin round as he touched her shoulder.

'Towel?'

She caught the one he threw her neatly, watching him warily.

'You and me need to have a little chat.'

'What about? And shouldn't it be you and I?'

He was impressed by the way she'd so quickly recovered herself. But it wouldn't do.

'You have a good brain, Cristyne,' he said, lounging against the cooker.

'Yes. Good eyesight, too.' She stared at him unflinchingly. 'Is that what you want to talk to me about? What I saw last night?'

'You saw nothing! Just my secretary and I off for dinner after a long day in which we'd both worked through lunch.'

He took a step forward, spitting out the words, unleashing the fury her insolence provoked in him. She flinched, lowering her eyes and gripping the towel, waiting for him to finish. He heard the bath emptying, footsteps as the boys clambered out of the bath. Time was against him but already he knew he'd beaten her down.

He took a step back, the civilised barrister once more, basking still in the power that watching her cower had lent him.

'I trust I've clarified this point with you.'

He spoke to her as if she were a client and enjoyed the irony.

'Of course,' she said, meek and obedient once more, which was exactly how he liked his women.

'Now, I'm going to the lounge to get myself a much needed drink.' His eyes scoured the mess piled up on the kitchen surfaces. 'So I'll leave you to your chores.'

His eyes alighted on the kitchen knife. Wicked, he knew, but he simply couldn't resist it.

'Don't forget to put the knives away, will you? It would be terrible if there were an accident.'

Then he turned and, still buzzing with adrenaline, made his way to the lounge. He didn't see Cristyne staring after him, with hate-filled eyes.

2

Kieran had his reasons for volunteering to take Erin with him to pick up his mother-in-law.

With Erin gurgling away in her baby seat behind them, all starfish waves and cute burps, he could tell Grace the latest village news without alarming her. One gummy smile from Erin and Granny would turn gaga like she always did, allowing Kieran to move on to more cheerful topics. That was what he hoped, at least.

Now, on the return journey, he was nervously putting his theory to the test. So far it seemed to be working.

'Of course, the attempted break-in came as a shock,' he said. 'But thankfully, whoever it was didn't manage to get in. Too impatient, the police said. Plenty more places to try. As Stevie said, we were lucky.'

Translation: *You said Quantock-cum-Steeple was virtually crime free. That was how you managed to persuade me to leave my job, my friends and my home and allow myself to be dragged all the way out here to the sticks.* All this accompanied by mounting rage, tears and cushion-throwing. Not good, and though Stevie was now actually talking to him again — kind of — things hadn't improved all that much since.

Kieran hated it when Stevie got low. He couldn't help it but he always felt like it was his fault and he'd let her down. And Stevie and Erin were the two people he feared letting down the most. He'd taken a big risk setting up on his own as a graphic designer after years of drowning in tides of corporate misery. Often, since he'd taken the decision, he lay awake at night, haunted by the thought that Stevie had finally realised he wasn't a deity but a mere mortal and a flawed one, too. He dreaded the day arriving when his daughter came to the same realisation, and already he felt the pain of it like a blow to the heart.

'Burglaries happen everywhere these days,' Grace said. 'I'm glad Stevie seems to be taking it philosophically.'

'Oh, absolutely!' He decided it was time to change the subject. 'Did she tell you she'd met someone with a baby Erin's age? And then there's Margaret, our neighbour. In fact, it's because of Margaret that I'm here and not Stevie. Fell off a ladder.'

'Oh dear. How awful for her!'

'Margaret not Stevie, obviously.' Kieran, grinning inanely at this remark, was aware he was wittering on but seemed powerless to stop. 'Stevie's off visiting her in hospital.'

'Oh, good! I must say the move seems to be working out very nicely.' Grace sat back and contemplated the view for the first time. 'You definitely made the right decision moving here, Kieran. So peaceful after London and so much less stressful.'

'Yeah, right,' Kieran mused, losing himself in his own far from stressless thoughts as Grace launched into a long tale about what had happened to her on her journey.

Grace could never just get on a train at one end and get off at the other without having an adventure. Life, for her, was one opportunity after the next to make new friends, or come to the aid of strangers or witness an event that sooner or later would become public knowledge and entail her making a statement to the authorities.

'I'm just a Nosey Parker,' Grace had gone on public record as saying, after the time she felled a would-be shoplifter in John Lewis with her brolly. 'Just never got the hang of keeping myself to myself.'

'Home at last,' Kieran said, some fifteen minutes later as they turned into Pleasant Grove.

'Extraordinary, don't you think, some people's behaviour these days? And right in the middle of a busy platform where everybody could see what was going on, too!'

'Absolutely,' Kieran said.

Though, actually, he hadn't heard a word she'd said.

★   ★   ★

Margaret wasn't expecting Stevie. She was in a side ward, the dimple-cheeked nurse said, but perhaps Stevie might think about grabbing herself a coffee first before popping in to see her, as she already had company. Her son, probably, she added, before rushing away.

Though the coffee had been undrinkable, Stevie had enjoyed sitting in the cafeteria and watching the world go by. Hobble and limp in one or two cases, too. Since Erin's arrival her life had taken on a manic quality that didn't really suit her dreamy nature.

In the middle of a must-do chore, something small and time-wasting would distract her. Searching for the cheese grater she'd last seen a week ago, for instance, or letting her eyes rest a few minutes too long on a pair of robins exchanging gossip on the wall. For the rest of the day, no matter how hard she ran to catch up with herself, she never quite made it. The end result, according to her mother at least, was a household system that bordered on anarchy.

It was nice to put a bit of distance between herself and Kieran too. Things had been awkward between them since she'd blamed him for the attempted break-in. He was still smarting from her attack, she knew, but she wasn't quite ready to say sorry yet.

Crushing the Styrofoam cup in her hand, she wondered briefly how on earth they were going to keep this lack of marital harmony from her mother.

⋆　⋆　⋆

'I must say I found it difficult to believe at first, Stevie, you visiting a neighbour in hospital. But I'm really pleased you're coming out of your shell at last.'

They were tucking into the cake that Grace had whipped up just before she'd left home. Iced ginger, one of Stevie's childhood favourites. She'd hugged her mother tightly when Grace brought it out of the tin, an uncharacteristic action on Stevie's part that had flustered Grace, prompting her to tell her daughter not to be so silly, it was only a cake.

Stevie couldn't have explained why she'd acted that way. Perhaps it was the Proustian effect — with ginger cake instead of madeleines. All her childhood memories flooding back suddenly, making her wonder what on earth she was doing with a house, a husband and a child when really she was only a little girl herself. What were madeleines, anyway?

Kieran was being so sweet to her right now in front of Mum. Truth was she was beginning to feel slightly ashamed of herself for the way she'd behaved towards him. The break-in had no more been Kieran's fault than it had been hers and it wasn't as if he'd dragged her to Quantock-cum-Steeple against her will either, whatever she'd claimed on the spur of the moment when she'd been upset. He'd suffered enough this past week, she decided.

'Did Kieran tell you he's got his first client? When they see how brilliant he is they'll send plenty more business his way, for sure,' she said.

There, that hadn't been too difficult, had it? Her ringing endorsement of her husband's talent was rewarded by a gratified smile from Kieran, despite his mouth being full of cake.

'Dark horse,' Grace said. 'He was too busy telling me about what you were up to to talk about himself. Making new friends and so on.'

'Oh, that.'

Stevie didn't want to talk about Alana. She felt a bit of a fool, actually, investing so much meaning into one visit to her house for a cup of coffee and a shared packet of croissants. Phoning her up to tell her of the attempted break-in, then leaving some garbled hysterical message when Alana failed to pick up the phone. Hardly surprising she hadn't called back.

Although maybe when she'd rung again a couple of days later, leaving yet another message, the least Alana could have done was to ring back — even if it was to make some excuse about being too busy to meet up right now. Stevie wasn't stupid. She'd have taken the hint.

Perhaps Kieran was right and Alana in her large home was simply out of Stevie's league. Maybe there was some sort of secret code of conduct people in big houses with au pairs lived by that simply by-passed the social circles in which Stevie usually mixed. Well, what-ever, she wouldn't be ringing her again. If Alana wanted to get back in touch then she knew her number.

Erasing Alana from her mind, Stevie explained the circumstances that had landed her neighbour in hospital, adding she'd only gone along to see her because she felt guilty for not having offered to get up the ladder to trim back the greenery for Margaret herself.

'But that's nonsense,' Grace said. 'You hardly have the time to do your own outdoor jobs, let alone take on your next-door-neighbour's.'

Stevie and Kieran exchanged guilty-as-charged faces, both hugely relieved that, though no words had been spoken, their quarrel, such as it had been, finally appeared to be over.

'People do rather keep themselves to themselves round here,' Kieran said. 'In fact, what was that bet you wanted to have with your mum, Stevie? A bottle of the village store's finest vintage if Grace manages to wangle an invitation inside Margaret's house while she's here, wasn't it?'

'Done,' Grace said, holding out her hand to shake on it. 'I'll start as soon as she gets back from the hospital.'

'They're letting her out tomorrow, apparently. But frankly, Mum, I don't think you've got a prayer,' Stevie said, proffering her own hand in return. 'Nice as pie when I went to visit her but — well — hospital's neutral territory, isn't it?'

'Making friends just takes time, that's all,' Grace said. 'Tell me, does she have any family, this Margaret?'

Stevie shrugged. 'Like I said, I haven't managed to get much out of her all the time we've been here. She did have a visitor before me. Her son, the nurse thought. But when I mentioned it to Margaret she said she had no son. Swore she'd been sleeping till five minutes before I turned up so if anyone had been at her bedside then she hadn't noticed them. Got a bit irate about it, actually.'

'How do you mean, irate?'

Stevie could practically see her mother's nose quiver with curiosity.

'Now, Mother dearest, please don't go all Miss Marple on me, will you? This isn't St Mary Mead and Margaret isn't harbouring some dark secret.'

'Honestly, Stevie. You're just like your father. Anything for a quiet life, the pair of you. I tell you, if I was conducting a passionate affair on the breakfast table he wouldn't remove his nose from the *Telegraph*.'

'Mum! Please!'

'Well, it's obvious to me anyway. Why would a mother publicly deny her own flesh and blood?'

Kieran and Stevie exchanged nonplussed glances.

'Because she's ashamed of him, that's why. You can bet he's let her down in some way. And I expect he's done it several times, too. Mothers don't give up on their children all that easily, you know, Stevie. As you'll find out for yourself sooner or later. Now, who's for another bit of cake?'

'It's so nice to see you again, Mum,' Stevie said, holding out her plate. 'I wonder what we did for excitement till you arrived.'

★　　★　　★

The first time Edgar had cheated on her she hadn't seen it coming. Pregnant with their first child, Alana had been wrapped up in her own little bubble and had simply put Edgar's mysterious phone calls and late nights down to work.

The second time she'd recognised the signs. But by now she had a toddler and a teething infant to consider. She'd gritted her teeth and waited for it to pass, consoling herself with the fact that Edgar had too much to lose to let it go on. This house was in her name, thanks to her father, and she had the children, of course, her ultimate weapon on the battlefield of a difficult marriage.

Now she was almost certain history was repeating itself for a third time. He was behaving oddly, spending too much time looking in the mirror and choosing his ties. Disappearing for a whole morning when he should have been at work and quite unable to give a coherent explanation other than to say he'd had stuff on.

But far from venting her fury on him,

Alana was reserving most of her loathing for herself. What was the matter with her that she was prepared to put up with his behaviour like some downtrodden little woman whose only option in life was to stand by her man no matter what? And now here she was, on her knees, sorting through his washing as if it were all she was good for.

She blamed Stevie for making her feel so unsettled. Sitting in her kitchen, her chin smeared with jam, Stevie's face had lit up at the mere mention of her own husband's name.

When Stevie left, Alana found herself dwelling on the lack of support Edgar offered these days. It felt bitter to acknowledge it, but it was impossible, once she'd started, to shy away from powerful feelings she'd suppressed for so long. It wasn't just his emotional neglect she felt. He did nothing practical with the children or in the house. It was her father, popping in unexpectedly one day and catching her at her lowest ebb, who'd insisted she should have some domestic help.

She'd welcomed Cristyne like one of the family, but all Edgar had done was treat her like a slave. She found herself thinking again of the night she'd left the boys asleep after their bath to come downstairs to ask Cristyne something. Thinking she'd heard raised voices coming from the kitchen, she'd stopped on the stairs to listen.

Edgar had come strolling out of the kitchen heading for the lounge, the same supercilious grin on his face as he wore when he thought he'd got the better of someone — usually her — in an argument.

She'd left it a moment before going into the kitchen. Cristyne was at the sink, her headphones in her ears, so failed to hear Alana approach. But as soon as Alana put out her hand to touch her shoulder, she'd spun round, an expression of fear on her face.

'Oh, it's you,' she'd said, as she'd relaxed.

What had Edgar done to her to make her fear him so? she'd wondered since.

The following morning Cristyne announced she'd had a weekend invitation from her cousin, an au pair like herself, in London. She'd pinned up a piece of paper with the address and landline number of where she'd be staying and that was that.

That had been nearly a week ago and she hadn't even rung to explain why she hadn't returned when she said she would. When Alana told Edgar she thought they'd seen the last of Cristyne, all he'd said was good riddance to bad rubbish. But he wasn't the one who'd been left in the lurch. She'd better get on. If Edgar didn't have a clean shirt for tomorrow there'd be hell to pay.

★ ★ ★

'Of course! Now I remember where I've seen her before!' said Grace.

Stevie, Grace and the baby were strolling round the village pond. Ducks quacking, willows weeping, spring flowers bending in the breeze. It was all there. Stevie had been adjusting Erin's bonnet as Grace spoke, crouching down by the buggy and thinking how cute her daughter looked in her cream, fur-trimmed, quilted all-in-one ensemble, like a miniature skier.

'Say again?' said Stevie.

'The girl I saw on the station platform, arguing with that man.'

'Oh, that.'

'You know how it is when you see someone out of context and you can't place them? Well, it's been puzzling me all this time. But being back in the same place has jogged my memory. Last time I visited, you see, when you'd just moved, I brought Erin out on this same walk. I bumped into her — the girl — while feeding the ducks with the children, just like we're doing now. We had a lovely long chat.'

Stevie didn't want to say she'd met Alana's au pair, too. When Grace had urged her to say more about the new friend Kieran had mentioned, she'd quickly explained it away by saying he'd got the wrong end of the stick and that just because they'd exchanged greetings in the shop it didn't make them friends. Her mother had given an understanding sigh and returned to her favourite topic — how forward her granddaughter was — and the subject, thankfully, was dropped for good.

'Actually, looking back, I can't help wishing I'd done something about what I saw on the platform,' Grace said. 'She looked quite shaken, actually. Pushing the man away. Quite desperate.'

'Really? And did no one do anything?'

'No one ever does these days, do they? Too afraid of how it might turn out. Though if the train hadn't left when it did I certainly would have intervened. Jumped off and given him a piece of my mind, without a thought for the consequences.'

Stevie tucked her arm through her mother's, in a protective gesture.

'I bet you would, too, though I do wish you'd stop interfering in other people's problems, Mum.'

'I don't interfere,' Grace protested. 'I merely observe. It's just that sometimes I can't help, you know . . .'

'Interfering?' Stevie grinned. 'So, what do you think was going on between them? You never really said.'

'I did, dear, but I think you may have been dozing at the time.'

'Was I? Blame Erin for that. Anyway, I'm awake now, so go on.'

'Well, it looked to me like he was trying to make her go with him and she wasn't having any. She ran off, he followed and that was when the train pulled out. She may have jumped on it and got away from him completely. For my own peace of mind I just wish I could be a bit more sure about that.'

'What did this bloke look like?'

'He had his back to me so I couldn't see his face.'

'Oh, well, I wouldn't worry about it. She'll be back au pairing by now, I shouldn't wonder,' said Stevie.

Her phone was ringing. Kieran probably, she decided. But it was Alana's name that had flashed up on her screen. Putting the phone to her ear, she expected small talk, an apology for the delay in getting back to her, anything but what she got.

'Mum, would you mind taking Erin home on your own? Only, someone — well, I guess you'd call her a friend — has asked how quickly I can be at her house.'

* * *

The kitchen at Alana's house was very different from the last time she'd been there. It looked remarkably similar to Stevie's, in fact. Alana, oblivious to the mess, sat clutching a man's shirt in both hands, staring straight ahead.

She couldn't face the playground, she said, and hoped Stevie didn't think it a cheek calling her to ask her if she wouldn't mind collecting the children instead. Naturally, in the circumstances, Stevie had agreed.

For more than two hours, over pints of coffee, she'd sat and listened to Alana's story of previous betrayals and present suspicions, culminating in the evidence before them. The oldest cliché in the book. Lipstick on the collar. She wished Alana would put the stained shirt away, but it was as if she needed to hold on to it physically, to support the decision she'd just made — that this time, her marriage was over.

The mess in the kitchen reminded her of Cristyne's absence and after the conversation she'd just had with her mother it worried her. She guessed there'd be no point raising the subject with Alana, however. She was clearly in the process of summoning all her energy for a showdown with Edgar and could think of nothing else. She'd rung him at work. Ordered him home, she said, widening her eyes at the word. She'd never ordered Edgar to do anything before and it felt good, she said.

But it was no use — Stevie couldn't put the subject of Cristyne aside. Tentatively she mentioned her name. Where was she? And when was she coming back?

'She said she was visiting her cousin in London for the weekend,' said Alana. 'She was meant to be catching the train that would have got her in at midday. Four days ago.'

Grace's train. She hadn't imagined it then. Not that she'd ever really doubted her mother's sharp eyes.

'I don't suppose she will come back now.' Alana sighed. 'Damn Edgar!'

'Edgar? What does he have to do with it?'

'Oh, he was always having a go at her. She was terrified of him, poor thing. And Edgar enjoyed terrifying her, too. The night before she left I overheard something in the kitchen. The following day she mentioned the cousin.'

Stevie was beginning to feel distinctly uneasy at this turn of events.

'You think she was running away from him?'

Tugging at the shirt collar on her lap, Alana shrugged.

It was no use; Stevie could hold the story in no longer. Hesitantly, she recounted the scene that Grace had witnessed on the station platform. Alana said nothing till Stevie finished. When she finally did speak, her voice was cold and her glare unflinching.

'I don't know what you're suggesting about my husband, but I think you should leave right now. I'll pick the children up myself after all, thank you.'

Stevie, realising she'd crossed the line for the second time with Alana, tried to make amends, protesting that she hadn't meant to offend her and she couldn't think why she'd spoken as she had.

But Alana wasn't even looking at her any more. There was nothing that she could do to put this right, Stevie knew. Quickly, she stumbled out of the kitchen and let herself out of the house.

Alana let go of the shirt at last. Stevie was talking rubbish. Why would Edgar want to do any physical harm to Cristyne? He wasn't the type. Words were his weapons. But all the same. Maybe she should just have a quick look at the piece of paper Cristyne had pinned up. She hadn't been answering her own phone. Maybe the cousin or the lady of the house had a better idea of Cristyne's whereabouts.

But no matter for how long she scoured the board, she couldn't see it anywhere. Someone had removed it. And, as the soft purr of Edgar's Merc reached her ears, her heart contracted with fear.

3

The first time Grace had attempted to wangle an invitation inside Margaret's house, she hadn't even opened the door, although Grace could have sworn she'd spotted a twitching curtain at an upstairs window. To give Margaret the benefit of the doubt, she *had* only just got back from hospital and had probably been advised to rest, so, undaunted, Grace vowed to return next day.

At least this time Margaret appeared. It was very kind of Grace to call round and ask if there was anything she could do, she said, but actually she'd been allocated a home help temporarily so, really, she was fine. Grace hovered a bit longer, explaining how Stevie had wanted to come herself, but was worried that baby Erin's presence might be a bit much for Margaret so soon after her accident, which was why Grace was here instead. But no amount of hovering gained her admission. Margaret was expecting the nurse any minute, she explained. Maybe another time. Not even Grace — who'd never been shy at coming forward — felt able to push it any further and ask *when*, exactly, this other time would be.

Trilling a cheery farewell, she'd walked backwards down the drive, waving all the way. Unfortunately, she drifted off course somewhat, like some wayward hot-air balloon, and ended up in the privet hedge, wondering what it was about Margaret Bradley that made her feel like a foolish schoolgirl.

Despite this setback, here she was for the third time. She'd taken on this bet with Stevie and was determined to win it — a bottle of the village store's finest vintage if she got herself invited inside Margaret's house. Having more or less suggested that Stevie simply wasn't in the same league as herself when it came to making friends, it was now a matter of pride to prove it.

In addition, she was determined to get to the bottom of Margaret's denial that she had a son, even though Stevie had seen someone the right age to qualify as one, at the end of her hospital bed. There was bound to be some evidence of him in Margaret's house. All she needed was to get to the bottom of it and she'd be proved right. Though what she would do with this evidence, she hadn't a clue, not quite having got to that bit yet.

One thing was certain: her desire to get her foot in Margaret's door had nothing to do with the alcohol Stevie was offering as a prize. She'd paid enough visits to the village shop to see for herself the sorry state of affairs it was in. Little surprise it was up for sale. The wine on offer at that place barely merited tipping into a spag bol, let alone a glass.

As she'd mentioned to Stevie only yesterday, whoever took that dump on would have to be possessed of a great deal of enthusiasm if they hoped to persuade all those customers who'd deserted them for the out-of-town supermarket to return.

Stevie had launched into an explanation of how exactly *she* would run the shop if it were hers. Grace had been quite bowled over by her enthusiasm — she hadn't seen Stevie so fired up in a long time. Maybe she had a bit more of her own get-up-and-go than she'd so far acknowledged. Pity she hadn't married a wealthy man, though, who could finance all those excellent ideas that she'd come up with. But Stevie had married for love, bless her, not financial security.

And Kieran was a lovely man. 'You go and win your bet, Grace,' he'd said just now. 'I'll take Erin for a stroll while Stevie's off sorting her friend out. Might as well take advantage of being self-employed, eh?'

A proper twenty-first century man, he was. As far removed from Stevie's father, who wouldn't have known one end of a baby from the other, as could be.

Through the small circle of coloured glass above the door, she saw Margaret's white hair first before the rest of her followed. Grace patted her own professionally tinted locks and arranged her smile. There was much jangling of keys before finally the door was opened.

'Chocolate orange,' Grace said, whipping the green-and-white chequered cloth from the plate she extended. 'Irresistible.'

There was a flicker of something like resistance in Margaret's watery blue eyes but it didn't last long.

'You'd better come in,' she said grimly. 'I'll put the kettle on.'

To Grace's delight and relief, with every bite, Margaret appeared to thaw another fraction of a degree. Not that she was exactly exuding warmth as she complimented Grace on the cake, then proceeded to fill her in on her experience at the hospital — in particular, the dire quality of the food — but exuberance was obviously not in Margaret's nature. Not everyone was as chatty as she was herself, Grace knew.

As she sipped her tea, she glanced surreptitiously around the room, looking for clues. There were none. Not a single photo on the wall, or mantelpiece, or chest of drawers. It was definitely odd. The time had come for a few leading questions.

Margaret managed well by herself, that much was obvious, she said. But it wasn't easy growing older on one's own, was it?

Speaking for herself, she couldn't help wishing sometimes that she lived a bit nearer to Stevie than she did. Since she'd retired, she'd begun to feel so out of touch with the modern world. (A lie, actually, as the first thing she'd done when she retired was buy herself a laptop and an iPod, then proceeded to pester her neighbours' children till they'd taught her to become a wizard with both.)

If she'd hoped for some sort of revelation about a son — or a husband, come to that — she got nothing. Margaret would only say that she'd been on her own for more years than she cared to remember, that she was used to it and that, actually — with a glance at the clock — she enjoyed her own company.

Grace knew a hint when she heard one dropped. Obviously, she would be going home empty-handed. If she could only have one last little look round. This Margaret was a dark horse if ever she'd met one, and now she'd got the bit between her teeth. Her own teeth, obviously, not Margaret's.

Offering sticky hands as an excuse,

Grace mounted the creaky stairs to the little bathroom. 'No need to show me where it is,' she insisted. 'This house is a mirror image of Stevie and Kieran's.' With the added difference that in Margaret's house you could actually see the floor below, instead of feeling like you'd embarked on an assault course as you negotiated scattered newspapers, empty mugs and baby clutter just to get from one side of the room to the other.

A quick splash at the sink and Grace was out on the landing again. She knew there must be two bedrooms and the bigger one in which Margaret would most likely sleep would be at the back of the house. She wouldn't be missed for another couple of minutes at least. Plenty of time to pop inside and have a peek.

She was disappointed. Apart from a mirror on the wall and a couple of landscapes above the bed, nothing. Not even a framed photo on the bedside table. The small room then. It wouldn't hurt to pop her head round the door.

Skipping across the landing, she slipped into the smaller bedroom — this one facing the front garden. A police car drove sedately by — a far cry from the seventy-mile-an-hour speed dashes she was used to witnessing in her neck of the woods. Probably on their way home for lunch, Grace decided.

It was then her eyes alighted on the single bed, with its Aston Villa bedcover. More Villa paraphernalia about the room — a scarf, a signed photo of the team next to the bed. On the wall, a film poster. She recognised it — *Trainspotting*. And next to that, a photograph of a rather beefy young man with big ears, dressed in hoody and trainers, patting the head of an equally beefy dog with equally big ears. Both appeared equally unlovable, too, for that matter, scowling at the camera in a most unnerving manner, Grace thought.

Margaret may have been a heavy woman, but she was light on her feet. Or maybe she knew where exactly on the stairs to stand so they wouldn't creak. Now she hovered in the doorway, accusing Grace with her whole body.

'Oh, dear,' Grace said. 'I must have taken a wrong turning.'

★   ★   ★

Stevie had finally stopped crying. But only after dire warnings from an unusually subdued Grace about what it would do to her milk if she carried on.

'What must Alana think of me?' Stevie blew her nose hard. 'She asked me over to listen to her suspicions that he is having an affair, and what did I do instead? Only suggest she could take her pick as to whether her husband was guilty of assault, murder or kidnap of their own au pair. Or possibly all three.'

'I'm sure it wasn't really like that, dear.'

'I didn't mean it like that, but that's definitely how she took it.'

'People can be very funny when it comes to listening to criticism about their loved ones,' said Grace sagely.

Grace had given the impression of listening hard to Stevie's story at first, but halfway through, she'd started to fidget — something Stevie had found distracting and just the teeniest bit annoying, actually.

'Anyway, where were you just now

while I was here sobbing into my hankie?' she asked.

She'd been visiting Margaret, she said, avoiding Stevie's eyes.

'In her house?'

Grace nodded. Her lack of any display of triumph troubled Stevie. She seemed miles away.

'So, you've won the bet then!'

Her mother waved her hand. 'No, really. Forget it. Honestly,' she mumbled.

'OK, Mother. Come on. What's up?' Stevie demanded. 'Because something definitely is, for sure.'

Grace seemed relieved to be able to confess at last. She'd been caught snooping by a furious Margaret, she said. Just as Stevie was poised to admonish her for abusing Margaret's hospitality, Grace stopped her in her tracks.

'Listen to what she told me first, then tell me what you think we should do,' she said urgently. 'She said her son, Darren, has been in prison. For robbery and theft. Three times. That he just got out. And that it was him who pushed her off the ladder and caused her accident in the first place.'

'No way!'

'He was after money from his mother, apparently, but she refused point blank to hand it over,' Grace added.

Cogs began to turn in Stevie's brain. That explained their burglary that day.

'So he knocked her off the ladder, came running round to our place and attempted to punch his way into our house through the conservatory window!'

Grace nodded. 'I think there's something else, too,' she said urgently. 'The au pair and the man on the platform. I think it might have been him.'

'What? How can you be sure?' Stevie said. 'You said you didn't see his face.'

'I know,' Grace admitted. 'But there was something about his stance. And that close-shaven head. And a hoody. Yes, I'm sure he was wearing a hoody.'

'Even Dad wears a hoody,' Stevie said. 'Tell me someone who doesn't wear a hoody these days.'

Even as the words escaped, she already knew the answer. Edgar Ford didn't wear a hoody. He wore Savile Row suits for work, and Pringle sweaters and Daks chinos at the weekend.

'Oh, blimey,' she said. Not exactly her swear word of choice, but Grace didn't approve of that particular one.

'You need to inform Alana that there may very well be something to worry about where her au pair is concerned,' Grace said.

'But it's Darren, not Edgar, who's the danger,' said Stevie.

Given that she had not long ago been thrown out of Alana's house, it was only by extracting a commitment from Grace to accompany her back there that she agreed to return.

As the two women approached the Fords' house, two police officers, one male, one female, climbed into their car, which was parked outside. Stevie and Grace exchanged cautious glances.

'Oh, my God! What if she's shopped Edgar?' Stevie said. 'She must have sat there deliberating over my words and come to the conclusion that all that nonsense I came out with about him being in some way responsible for Cristyne's disappearance was correct. Maybe those policemen are even now on their way to intercept him and arrest him!'

'Well, if that's the case, then we need to put Alana right immediately.'

'If I hadn't wasted so much time feeling sorry for myself you could have told me all this sooner and we'd have got here before the police,' Stevie said.

'Getting things off your chest is never a waste of time,' Grace said. 'And if you can't have a good sob in front of your mother, then who can you do it in front of?'

She marched brusquely up the drive towards the house, Stevie following reluctantly behind. Alana could only have thought the police had forgotten something and returned, she surmised, or she wouldn't have answered the door so quickly. As soon as she realised that it wasn't them but Stevie, who appeared to have brought along protection this time, her face closed up.

'I've come to apologise, Alana,' Stevie said, all in a rush. 'So please, if you can find it in your heart to forgive me . . . '

Alana stood back from the door and held it open.

'Come in,' she said wearily. 'You'll be glad to know I took your advice.'

Grace practically fell over the threshold in her eagerness to get inside. Stevie was more reluctant, given that it seemed as if Alana had just shopped her own husband to the police and all because *she* — Stevie — had got the wrong end of the stick.

'Oh, dear,' she said. 'I think I've got some explaining to do.'

'Let *me* do it,' Grace said, in an attempt to soften the blow.

★ ★ ★

It had been foolishly optimistic on Cristyne's part to imagine she could cling to her story indefinitely. Her cousin, Wanda, had been suspicious right from the day she'd turned up on her doorstep unannounced and had grown more suspicious with every day that passed.

'I'm just not cut out for being an au pair,' was all Cristyne told her initially. 'I miss home. Far too much to stay in the UK any longer.'

'But what about all those letters you

sent me telling me just how well you fitted in?' a clearly puzzled Wanda wanted to know.

'I know, I know,' Cristyne said. 'I thought if I wrote it often enough, I might believe it.'

If Wanda had felt the urge to probe further she held back. Cristyne was welcome to stay a few days, she said, while the parents of the children she looked after were away in Paris for a romantic break, but then she'd have to get the train back to Quantock-cum-Steeple and inform the Fords of her decision that she was flying home.

'But I can't do that,' Cristyne wailed. 'There's no way I can ever go back there again.'

Even then Wanda didn't pry, although she did put her foot down about her cousin's obligations. Wanda was big on obligations. When her year as an au pair came to end, she was all set to embark on her degree in international Politics, so that, once qualified, she'd be in the best position to take herself off to some developing country to 'do good'. You couldn't talk about running away from your responsibilities to someone like Wanda, Cristyne should have realised.

But on the day that Darren, the lad she'd met in the village pub, turned up at the house looking for her, things changed. Wanda declared she'd had enough of Cristyne's dissembling. And now, with this smudged photograph of her on the front page of the *Evening News* describing her as a missing person, Cristyne realised it was time to come clean.

'They're looking for a man in connection with your disappearance,' Wanda said, scanning the words on the page. 'Someone has given an eyewitness account of an argument that took place on the station platform.'

That was the morning Cristyne finally caved in and agreed to return to Quantock-cum-Steeple, if only for the night. Darren had charmed her whereabouts from Wanda and managed to catch up with her, just as she'd been about to board the train. She'd fled from him, returning immediately to her cousin's house, where she'd finally spilled out the whole story.

Wanda had listened without passing any judgment. She could have said that Cristyne had been a fool to fall for Darren's flattery. She was no oil painting, after all. He'd wormed his way into her affections for one thing and one thing only — to sweet talk her into being his accomplice in a crime.

'He knew I knew the code for the Fords' burglar alarm,' she'd told Wanda. 'I knew when people were in and when they were out. I was there with a rag to wipe away fingerprints. He must have seen me coming.'

She'd been so naïve, she realised that now. The night she'd spotted Edgar Ford with that other woman, who had she shared the information with but Darren? All she'd been able to think about was Alana's feelings, but Darren had totally disregarded this aspect of the situation.

For him, Edgar's adultery had been simply an opportunity to substitute one crime for another. Blackmail was less messy than burglary, he'd said. With the added benefit that once money had been extricated, you were always in a position to go back for a top-up a few months down the line.

It was after this that Cristyne realised she had to get away. Darren was crazy and she'd misjudged him. She thought she'd seen the back of him, but he must have got Wanda's address from her phone and tracked her down that way. He was never going to leave her alone if she remained working for the Fords. She had no alternative, she was convinced, but to return home.

But, before she did, she came up with a plan to scupper both Darren's blackmail plot and any chance Edgar might think he had of getting away with his bit on the side.

Except that now she didn't feel so good about it, and it was because of what she'd done that she felt unable to ring Alana and tell her she was safe.

'You did what?' Wanda dropped the newspaper in shock.

'I smeared Edgar's collar with lipstick. So that he'd have no choice but to confess. I thought if Alana knew what Edgar was up to, then there would be no point Darren trying to blackmail him, would there?'

Wanda blinked in disbelief.

'But I know now I only did it for my own sake — to get back at Edgar for trying to terrify me into keeping quiet — not really to protect Alana at all.'

'I always thought you were the most interesting cousin,' Wanda said. 'Looks like I've been proved right, doesn't it?'

★　★　★

In reply to his query as to whether she'd just been visiting, Grace could have told the driver that yes, she had. But that as soon as their London house was sold, she and her husband would be returning for good, moving to a much smaller property in order to free up some capital so that their daughter could buy the village shop with her friend and business partner, and convert it from the dump it was into the thriving emporium that Quantock-cum-Steeple deserved.

But Stevie had made her promise not to say a word to a soul. Difficult, she admitted, as ever since Grace had told her that she'd been thinking of a way to help them financially and that it was a chance conversation about the village shop that swung it, Stevie hadn't stopped jumping on the spot with excitement.

Alana was as keen as she was — keener now she'd finally managed to kick every trace of Edgar out of the matrimonial home. But there was many a slip and neither of them wanted to jinx it. This wasn't London, remember, Grace was warned, where everyone you met was a stranger. In Quantock-cum-Steeple, a careless whisper uttered at the school gates at nine in the morning would be all over the village by lunchtime.

It would be hard for the two women, both saddled with small children, Grace knew. But Alana had persuaded Cristyne to come back as joint nanny, throwing in a substantial pay rise for good measure, and Margaret had offered her services where needed, in return for all the support that Grace, Stevie and Kieran had given her through the dreadful time she'd had with her son, Darren.

But he was safely in custody now for a couple of botched robberies. And, after Cristyne had let it be known his part in her sudden disappearance from the village, and after Margaret herself had — albeit reluctantly — reported Darren for pushing her off the ladder, it would be a cold day in hell before that particular young man ever graced the narrow streets of this village again.

'So, it's back to the smoke for you then?' the taxi driver asked her.

'That's right,' she said. 'My son would have driven me, but he's at the other end of the country himself today, visiting clients. He's just set up his own business, so he has to take the work while he can. And my daughter . . . '

Oops! She was going to have to watch herself!

'Your daughter?'

'At home with the baby,' she said 'Teething. Up all night. I couldn't ask her to get behind a wheel.'

'Very wise. So,' said the driver. 'How did you find our little village?

'Charming,' Grace said. 'Quite delightful.'

'Expect it'll be a relief to get back to the city, though, won't it?' he said. 'I mean, Quantock-cum-Steeple's nice enough, but there's never anything much happens from one week to the next.'

Grace rested her head on the back of her seat. Personally, she'd had more than enough excitement recently. She couldn't wait to tell the whole story to Stevie's father — missing au pairs, criminal sons, errant husbands. Oh, and the baby's new teeth, of course, mustn't forget them.

But what she most looked forward to was the thought of his familiar response to her story. It would sustain her on her journey home. The nod, the grunt, then the final retreat behind *The Telegraph* for the rest of the evening. Home, sweet home.

THE END

We do hope that you have enjoyed reading this large print book.

Did you know that all of our titles are available for purchase?

We publish a wide range of high quality large print books including:
Romances, Mysteries, Classics
General Fiction
Non Fiction and Westerns

Special interest titles available in large print are:
The Little Oxford Dictionary
Music Book, Song Book
Hymn Book, Service Book

Also available from us courtesy of Oxford University Press:
Young Readers' Dictionary
(large print edition)
Young Readers' Thesaurus
(large print edition)

For further information or a free brochure, please contact us at:
Ulverscroft Large Print Books Ltd.,
The Green, Bradgate Road, Anstey,
Leicester, LE7 7FU, England.
Tel: (00 44) **0116 236 4325**
Fax: (00 44) **0116 234 0205**